DARN WEEDS!

Crazy Tales from Your Local Nursery

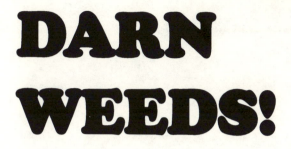

By
Don Urbanus

Illustrations by
Erin Urbanus

Darn Weeds! Crazy Tales from Your Local Nursery
by Don Urbanus

ISBN: 978-0-9968858-9-8
Library of Congress Control Number: 2018965368
Manzanita Writers Press
manzapress.com - manzanitawp@gmail.com

Author contact:
don@donsnursery.com
www.donsnursery.com

Cover Art, front & back – Erin Urbanus
Interior Illustrations: Erin Urbanus
Book Design & Layout: Joyce Dedini

Dedication

This book is dedicated to my wife, LeeAnne, who makes me complete. And to my daughter Erin, who I introduced to the world of comics and whose illustrations grace this book.

Introduction

Many of the stories in the book were originally included in newsletters, at first mailed out to customers, and then later in a digital format sent out over the years. It was time to get some of these stories into a book. The Quips and Questions were from notes taken down over many years by me or by some of the employees. They were stuffed in a file and came back to life when the book started. I would have gotten the collection out sooner, but I waited for my daughter to finish her art degree and get skilled enough to complete the illustrations. That's a good enough excuse as any.

Anyone can enjoy this book, but if you are a gardener or plant person, you will get an even bigger kick out of it. For some reason, I am in a lot of the stories. Of course, it's my nursery and my stories. I can guarantee one thing though—after this, you will never look at a nursery the same way again.

Table of Contents

Dedication   5
Introduction   7

Stories

Darn Weeds   11
Grafting Class   13
Get Fisbee!   17
Harvest Season   21
I Always Wanted to Work in a Nursery   24
The Patient   27
Galactic Nursery   30
The Great Employee   33
The Bug Blaster   36
The Ficus Tree   39
What's a Gophicula?   42
Christmas Eve   49
The Hungry Customers   53
The Garden of Eden   58
The Leafist   61
The Green Vote   69
The Tree Sale   72
Astrology for Plants   76
A Most Impressive Establishment   80
The Great Decline   83
The Truth about Snails   87
The Question   90

The Horticulturalist 94

The Fastest in the West 101

Any Complaints? 105

Plant Court Justice 107

The Last Nursery 113

Quips and Queries

Quips and Queries from the Nursery Trenches 116

I Love Working in a Nursery 117

Job Applicants 120

Do You Mind if I …? 122

Can You Get This? 124

People Unclear on the Concept 127

Are Tomatoes in Yet? 132

What's the Matter with My Plant? 133

Interesting Customers 137

That Costs Too Much! 142

Can I Get a Deal? 144

Angry Customers 146

Returns 148

Unanswerable Questions 151

Answerable but Silly Questions 154

Did You Really Do That? 161

You Can't Do That 166

Darn Weeds

Commander gliK stood in front of a light, soaking up the energy that was being absorbed into his green skin. With a flick of his tendril, he turned off the light and slithered into the command center. The new personnel officer, glaK, passed by, dragging a suggestive tendril under his chin. gliK almost burst his pollen sac and had to fight the urge to follow her through the door. He watched as she sauntered away. Turning around, he noticed his navigator grinning at him.

"Navigator gloK," he said, glaring. "Have you determined which planet might have intelligent life?"

gloK coughed and tried to suppress his smile. "Yes, I believe the third planet, Commander. At its position, the planet should be ideal for life as we know it."

"Are you suggesting there might be other kinds of life on this planet?" gliK asked cautiously.

"It's possible, Commander. We are receiving strange radio waves emanating from the planet but in such a variety of tones and sounds that the computer can't seem to decipher any of it. It assumes, therefore, that if there is life, they probably cannot communicate with each other."

The navigator listened into his headphone and then smiled. "Our science officer has just confirmed it. We have located intelligent life! And," gloK said, taking off his headphones, "it contains chlorophyll!"

Soon their spaceship was dropping down through wispy white clouds, and as the land appeared and the green creatures became more visible, they could hardly contain their excitement.

"Look," said gliK. "The green creatures must be highly advanced. Look how they have built monuments or structures for themselves. Navigator, steer the ship down to one of those buildings with lots of creatures."

"Yes, sir. Here's one," he said, squinting through his scope. "They seem to be having a meeting or gathering. There are thousands of individuals wearing some kind of black bottom. Lots of different sizes, too. Must be children and adults."

"Head for them," gliK said importantly. "Maybe they can take us to their leader. They might as well get used to the idea of us ruling their planet."

The spaceship landed next to a green-roofed building and the hatch flipped open. Commander gliK stood in the sunshine stretching his tendrils out. Such energy this sun gave! He crawled over to a huge rose bush that towered above him and held out a tendril in friendship—the other tendril held his ray gun. You couldn't be too careful with an inferior race.

Suddenly, without warning, Don bent down and grabbed gliK. "Darn weeds," he muttered. "What is this thing?" He tossed it into a bucket with the other weeds he had pulled, walked over to the compost bin and dumped them in. That was his third bucket of weeds. People had no idea that weeds were the biggest problem in a nursery—much more than insects or disease.

Navigator gloK slammed the hatch shut and zipped back into space. Personnel Officer glaK stroked Navigator gloK's shoulder with a thin green tendril.

"I guess this makes you the new commander," she purred.

gloK turned around, wrapped a tendril around glaK, and smiled wickedly.

Grafting Class

Vinny sat at the table polishing his brass knuckles while scanning through the local *Buy & Sell*. Every once in a while, he would make a comment about something being overpriced, or possibly stolen. He snorted and stifled a chuckle.

His boss, Big Lou, short for Luigi, glanced over at Vinny and rolled his eyes. Big Lou was a small-time crook but big on ambition.

"Hey, Vinny, why you waste your time lookin' through that rag, huh?"

"Take it easy, Boss. Sometimes you get good ideas. Look right here. This nursery here, Rising Sun Nursery, is givin' a class in graft. See here? It says: Learn How to Graft. And get this, it's free!"

Big Lou frowned, "What's the catch? Maybe those nursery guys mean somethin' else."

"Nah, Boss. Look right here. Websta's Dictionary says graft is, and I quote: the acquisition of gain in dishonest or questionable ways."

"What's questionable about it? They either pay up or we kills them."

"Boss, I think we should go down to that nursery. Maybe they is trying to cut into our territory."

"Now you's talkin', Vinny. Get my hat. We is going to have a little chat with Mr. Rising Sun Nursery Guy. Nobody cuts in on Big Lou."

Down at the nursery, there were a dozen green plastic chairs arranged in a semi-circle. The weather was crisp, but not too cold considering it was the end of winter. Don, the owner, had some 1-gallon trees and grafting compound on a cart. Multi-colored handouts were arranged on a small table. A half dozen people were already sitting. Some were reading the handouts about grafting or talking quietly among themselves.

Big Lou and Vinny, wearing pinstriped suits and fedoras, strutted up to the class, sizing up the people, and casing the nursery in general. Vinny pulled out a handkerchief and brushed it over one of the chairs. Big Lou grunted at Vinny and sat heavily down on the chair. Vinny kept standing, his legs spread wide, hands in his pockets. Occasionally he would look suspiciously around.

Don was about to welcome everyone to the class when Big Lou interrupted him. "Hey, Mr. Bigshot Nurseryman. How long you been doin' this graft thing?"

Don paused, looking at the unusual characters at his class. They didn't look like his typical nursery customers, but hey, who was he to exclude anyone? "It's been quite a few years now. I started doing it when—"

"Is that so?" Big Lou glanced back at Vinny who nodded in agreement. "And if you don't mind me bein' so bold, are you doing it right now?"

"Well," Don answered. "I do it this time of the year because that's when you do it. Things are slow and—"

Big Lou held up his stubby hand, "Hey, you's a business man. Ya gots to do what ya gots to do. Big Lou understands business. Don't I, Vinny?"

"Yes, you do, Boss," Vinny said, slowly and ominously.

"And, if you don't mind me asking, as one businessman to anotha, what exactly is your territory and how does ya do it."

"My territory?" Don asked. "You mean my customers?"

Big Lou grinned, "Sure, if you wanta call 'em that."

Don shrugged, "I guess mostly the tri-county area, but we do have customers from all over. Stockton, Sacramento, the Bay Area."

"I see," said Big Lou, tapping his fingers together rhythmically. "And your method?"

"Well, I use a knife like this one here. You can use most any knife as long as it is very sharp. A bevel on one side is the best."

"A knife," Big Lou repeated. "Hear that, Vinny? No noise. Leaves no trace." Vinnie nodded his head, impressed.

"Yes. And after a few years, you can't even tell where the cut was made. It heals over," Don agreed, smiling.

"You don't kill them?" Big Lou frowned.

"Well, you might lose a few here and there, but most are just fine.

You can make more money if they live, of course. And, I can save a lot of money doing it myself, too."

"Doing it myself," Big Lou echoed. With the last sentence, you could tell that the wheels were turning in Big Lou's head. He had a faraway look and then suddenly focused hard on Don. He stood abruptly and snapped his fingers. Vinny straightened up and stuck his hand inside his suit. Big Lou nodded his head at Don in respect.

"I'm sure we'll meet again, Mr. Rising Sun Guy. You gotta nice establishment here. Come on, Vinny. I seen enough."

On the way back to their car Vinny could hardly contain himself. "Say, Boss, you wants me to rub 'em out?"

Big Lou stopped at the car and gave Vinny a kiss on the cheek. "Vinny, Vinny. You gotta understand business, right? There's no hard feelings in business, am I right?"

"Sure, Boss."

"Vinny, let's take a ride down to the far side of Hogan Lake, way in the back. There's a special spot I wants to show ya." Hey, Big Lou thought, it's only business. That Mr. Bigshot Nurseryman showed him that.

Get Fisbee!

Professor Fisbee was elated. For years he had struggled as a virtual unknown in the world of plant genetics. Not anymore. He had somehow managed to survive budget cuts, downsizing, outsourcing, and mergers. Now finally, his experiments and perseverance had paid off. He would totally revolutionize the entire horticultural industry. A grateful world would immortalize him in the annals of genetic history.

He sat clutching his portfolio and waited in the plush office of Henry Greenwald, the CEO of Genetaplant, Inc. He had never met the CEO or anyone of any importance in the company. Fisbee smiled. It was a testament to the importance of his work that he was sitting here. A door opened and a tall, well-built man with graying temples stepped through.

"Professor Fisbee," he stated. "You can come in now."

"Mr. Greenwald?" Fisbee asked.

"You can call me Henry, Professor."

Fisbee stood up confidently, took in a big breath of air, and marched into the room. It was dark except for a large table in the middle of the room. The shades were drawn shut. Around the table sat a dozen very dour-looking men. They eyed him coldly. This immediately started Fisbee's heart pounding. Something was wrong. Wasn't he supposed to make his presentation to Mr. Greenwald?

"Gentlemen," said Greenwald, slowly scanning the room. "This is Professor Fisbee. Please tell these men what you told your supervisor yesterday, Professor."

"Well, I . . . I was saying," Fisbee stuttered. This isn't what Fisbee expected. He was expecting smiles, a ticker-tape parade, a big bonus, and congratulatory slaps on the back. Instead, the men sat there silently staring at him. He felt like a fish in a bowl monitored by a cat.

"Professor Fisbee? Please tell the—"

"Yes, of course," sputtered Fisbee. "My experiments. I have genetically manipulated plants so that they resist, I mean, they don't just resist, they don't get any diseases, or any bugs for that matter. Heat and cold don't bother them. Too much or too little water doesn't faze them. In fact, they don't die, period." Fisbee smiled. Now that he had said it, he felt much better.

"What do you mean *they don't die*," asked a portly man, choosing his words carefully and slowly. The others leaned forward expectantly.

Fisbee looked cautiously around the table. "They have been bred to live indefinitely. No disease kills or attacks them; no insects chew or suck them. Think what it will mean for the consumer," Fisbee added defensively. Why was he defensive? It was a wonderful idea. Think how much money the consumers would save.

"Professor?" asked Greenwald. "Who else knows about this, and where are your records?"

"Well, I have these, of course," Fisbee said, holding up his portfolio. "And my computer, naturally. Possibly an assistant or someone at the company's greenhouses knows about my work."

Someone sitting in the shadows got up quietly and left the room.

"These men here are giants in their field of business," Greenwald began slowly and thoughtfully. "They represent billions of dollars in our economy. In fact, they *are* the economy. What would happen to Smackum Industries if plants didn't need any fungicide or insecticide?"

The portly man glared at Fisbee. Others were frowning and hostile.

"And what about Growtech that makes plant growth regulators and rooting hormones? What about seed companies? What about the entire wholesale and retail nursery industry? If plants don't die or get diseased, what will they sell to the consumer?"

Numerous men around the table nodded their heads and there was a dark murmur of agreement.

"Plants have been good to us, Fisbee. We have been good for plants. Now you want to come in and change all that? Are you trying to destroy us?"

Fisbee was aghast. They weren't accepting his great scientific work. They wanted to stifle it. He was one of the greatest inventors and scientists of all time. He should be honored and placed on a pedestal alongside Newton, Galileo, Einstein, Marconi, and Edison. This couldn't be happening.

"Hand over your portfolio, Fisbee," Henry demanded. "It must be destroyed along with all of your records. It's for the good of the country—the world! We will compensate you, of course." The men in the room stood up, all eyes boring down on him.

Fisbee, wild-eyed, backed up, clutching his portfolio. "My work, my life's work!"

"Would a million take care of things? No? How about two million? Be a good fellow and hand it over now."

Suddenly, Fisbee made a dash for the door, and in a moment, he was running down the hallway. It was futile, Fisbee knew. His only hope were the few plants that he had given to Rising Sun Nursery, a retail nursery in the Sierra foothills. No one knew that he had given the owner a few experimental plants and Fisbee would never tell.

"Don't just stand there," yelled Greenwald. "Get Fisbee!"

Harvest Season

Don looked out the window at Rising Sun Nursery and saw the early morning sun splash oranges and reds across the Autumn Fantasy and Autumn Blaze maples. That meant one thing to Don. It was getting close for the fall harvest season and the cash register would be ringing.

He scanned the full assortment of firearms he had acquired for the harvest. It took a steady hand and a keen eye to shoot leaves while they were falling. That was the big challenge. Any idiot could get their quota of fall leaves by just shooting into the canopy of a tree. To get a big trophy leaf, blazing with color, with a bullet hole right in the middle of a leaf that had never touched the ground, well, that was a thing of beauty.

Don stroked the smooth contours of his most popular gun, the camouflaged Mossberg® 935 Magnum™ semi-automatic shotgun. In the nursery business, they called it "the Harvester." Don disdained that approach however. He preferred quality over quantity. He liked to pick the leaves off one at a time with a .22 rifle his father-in-law had given him. No scope, no night vision, not even semi-automatic, just a simple bolt-action .22 that had been used for fifty years or more.

He gazed at previous fall leaf trophies he had mounted on the walls of his store. It had been a stroke of genius to sell the trees that had garnered the most trophies. He even had mounted a rare Japanese maple "Emperor One" with a bullet hole right through the middle of the leaf. He remembered that one vividly. It took hours of patient waiting and focusing on that one leaf he knew was about to fall. The trick was to get it before it started sashaying in the wind on the way down to the ground. Bigger was not always better when it came to trophy harvesting.

Don had even started a website listing the places and times where wild leaves could be harvested. Of course, some Harvesters had their own secret tree sites and they were jealously guarded.

It was a wonderful time of the year, with the fall color, the holidays coming up, a faint wisp of smoke in the air, and the soft boom of shotguns and rifles in the distance.

Naturally, there were the protesters. Occasionally, the tree-huggers showed up and complained and held signs like "Let Nature Take its Course" or "Leaf the Trees Alone." Ridiculous. The trees were already letting go of their summer's work. So what if a Harvester took a trophy leaf here or there?

And there were always the complaints about stray bullets because Harvesters were shooting up into the air. Of course, there was always someone complaining about something.

Don sighed contentedly. Thanksgiving was coming up and he looked forward to it and a little recreational harvesting. He imagined that years from now he and his old friends would sit around and drink a toast to the leaf that got away.

I Always Wanted to Work in a Nursery

The judge looked down harshly at Don. "The defendant may rise. Do you have anything to say before the court passes sentence?"

Don stood up, conspicuous in an orange jumpsuit, and looked around. His mother was crying softly, her face buried in a tissue, but everyone else in the courthouse eyed him coldly.

"Your Honor, first, I would like to say that I'm sorry. I'd also like to explain the enormous pressure I was under running a nursery. You worry about the weather, the bugs, leaf-spot and mildew, weeds, watering the plants, staking and pruning, plants getting overgrown, plants too small. And everyone wants to talk to the owner to see if they can cut a deal. People want everything in bloom, even if the plants never get any flowers! They want plants that bloom or have fall color all year, that never need to be pruned or watered, that never get any bugs or ever have to be sprayed or fertilized." Don lifted his hands to explain and realized they were shackled. He sighed heavily. "When you take them all over the nursery to show them what might work for them, they pull out a catalog from some Midwestern company that sells little twiggy trees, and they point to a picture and want to know if we can get that tree or bush for them. The strain just got too much for me, your Honor. I . . . I'm sorry."

The judge smirked. "Oh, come now, Mr. Urbanus. You expect the court to believe that? Everyone knows how wonderful it is to work in a nursery. I myself would rather, well, never mind. In any case, you cold-bloodedly strangled that dear, sweet, little old lady and all she said to you was that she always wanted to work in a nursery. I'm sure that half the people in this court would also love to work in a nursery and fill the shoes you so despicably soiled. You are a disgrace to the nursery business. Therefore, I sentence you to twenty years to life in the nearest state penitentiary where I hope you will, at least, redeem yourself in the prison garden."

Don was led slowly away, chains dangling from his wrists and feet. By that afternoon he was shoulder to shoulder with other dangerous felons, issued his prison blues, and told to report directly to the warden.

The warden appeared pleased. "Says here you have a degree in horticulture. Very impressive. You used to work in a nursery?" the warden asked, not looking up from the papers on his desk.

"Yes, sir. I ran the entire operation," Don answered softly, his whole manner subdued and remorseful.

The warden gazed at Don with his cold blue eyes and thin lips, which were now breaking into a broad smile. "You know," said the warden thoughtfully. "I always wanted to work in a nursery."

Four guards had to pull Don off the warden.

The Patient

Dr. Don slowly and carefully pulled the green rubber gloves over his hands and held them up like a maestro. His patient would be there shortly. He was scrubbed and ready.

The ambulance screamed up to the emergency room and screeched to a halt. The driver, a burly man in his late twenties, ran around and opened the back of the ambulance. Inside, his partner, a petite blonde with a short no-nonsense haircut, held an I.V. The tube coiled down to the stretcher and disappeared under a blanket. They hurried the victim into the hospital where Dr. Don waited impatiently, frowning at them. He had lost two patients this weekend already and he didn't want to lose any more.

"What are the vital signs?" he asked, as he flipped the blanket off the patient.

The two paramedics locked eyes briefly. The petite blonde shook her head in silent knowing. In the real severe cases, she always did the talking, maybe because she was a little older than her partner, maybe because she had given natural birth to three kids. If a woman can do that and stay cool, she can do anything.

"Severe dehydration and no pulse, of course, Doctor."

"I can see that, Jenna, but why?" Dr. Don asked, exasperated. "Who is responsible for this patient?" he snapped. He didn't have time for lab tests and slow analysis from the pathology department. At their pace, the patient would be dead before he got any answers. He would have to use his gut feeling again.

As if on cue, a harried woman rushed into the room. Her hair was sticking up in places and she had a wild-eyed look. She choked on a sob.

"Is Binky okay?" she whimpered.

"Okay? Okay?" the doctor sneered. "Binky might not be long for this world." He looked at the patient's chart and then tossed it aside.

"As you can see, the patient is severely dehydrated, but the question is, why, Mrs. Thornstrom?"

"Well, I gave Binky water twice a week, but he started looking poorly so I started giving him water every day, and then I fertilized him to make sure he was getting enough nutrients. He started wilting, so I gave him some more water. Oh, Doctor, what did I do wrong? He was given to me by my last boyfriend. He just can't die!" She burst into tears.

"Mrs. Thornstrom," Dr. Don said, toning it down a bit. "You are killing your houseplant with kindness. The reason he is wilting is because his roots are rotting. No roots mean no water can get up to his leaves. Fertilizing him at this point is like trying to stuff a turkey dinner down a dying man's throat." Bending his head, he rubbed his brow with two fingers and a thumb. *Why can't they listen to their local nursery professional?*

At that point, the two paramedics left the room. It was out of their hands and they were needed elsewhere. Binky's life was now in the hands of one of the most skilled plant surgeons on the West Coast. A heavy-set nurse entered as they were leaving. She quickly came up to speed with the doctor. The doctor tapped the pot off the roots of poor Binky. A foul odor wafted into the air. He sighed and carefully knocked some soil off the roots. They were brown and discolored.

"Nurse, prepare a solution of ten percent Benlate. After surgery, we'll soak Binky in a three percent solution of hydrogen peroxide."

"Benlate, Doctor?" the nurse asked, handing him a towel to wipe his hands. "That fungicide is restricted. We can only use what's on the shelf and then there won't be any more. Is it that serious?"

Dr. Don just turned and glared at her.

"Yes, Doctor," said the nurse as she rushed out of the examining room.

Dr. Don turned and smiled at Mrs. Thornstrom, "Now, if you will just fill out these insurance forms."

"Don. Don!" Judy said, waving her hand in front of his face. "Are you daydreaming again? A lady brought a paper bag with a dried-up leaf in it. She wants to know what's wrong with her plant. Oh, and here's another one with a leaf with a hole in it. They want to know what bug made the hole."

Don sighed, removed the green rubber gloves and took the bags. He could spray the weeds later, he supposed. He opened the bag and frowned down at the leaf, wondering what it was.

Galactic Nursery

"I just love your nursery," she said as she gathered up her bag and took the receipt. "I tell all my friends about this place."

"Thank you. We appreciate that." I smiled as I opened the door for her. It was a busy Saturday. Sales were good. People were friendly. The sun was shining. Judy handed me the phone. "It's for you. Something about the CIA. I don't know. It's probably some crank call."

"Oh, boy," I muttered. It was most likely some salesman or someone wanting money for something. They usually didn't bother us on the weekend. I took the phone. "Hello?"

"Mr. Don Urbanus?" a gravelly voice asked.

"Who's calling?" I never answered yes to a telemarketer.

"Mr. Don Urbanus? Owner of Rising Sun Nursery?" He asked many personal questions, questions no regular person would know to ask.

"Who is this?"

"CIA. Just doing a background check. Would you consider yourself an expert on plants growing in tough hard rocky soil?"

His switch in questions caught me off guard.

"Well, I don't know about an expert, but we certainly have hard rocky soil in Calaveras County. At the nursery, we call our rocks 'Burson Potatoes.' We try to carry plants that grow well here, but they have to be *really* tough to survive in some of these soils, if you can call them that. I guess if you can grow them here you can grow them anywhere." With that, the phone clicked dead. No goodbye. Nothing. The crazy people that call a nursery.

A minute later, the phone rang again.

I picked it up. "Rising Sun Nursery."

"Is this Mr. Don Urbanus?" asked a soft southern feminine voice. Not another one.

"Speaking," I answered reluctantly.

"Hold on, sir. It's the President of the United States."

"What? Who did you—?" The phone clicked, and another voice came on.

"Hello, Don? This is the President. Your country needs you. Can I count on your help?"

"Um, sure. I guess so." I thought I'd play along with the joke. This probably had something to do with my friend, Chris, who lives in Mountain Ranch.

"To be blunt, Don, we're going to colonize Mars. We need people like you who can advise and supply the government with plants that will grow in those harsh Martian conditions. What I need from you is a list of plants that can grow in tough rocky soil. Are you onboard?"

"There is practically no atmosphere on Mars, Mr. President. Plants need air," I answered dryly.

"Plants need air? Are you sure? I thought they gave off oxygen! I'm going to have to investigate this. Maybe our intelligence is faulty somewhere."

"Besides," I continued. "Why ask me? There's a whole list of plants that can grow on Mars. It's all in the front of the Western Garden Book under Zones."

"Really? What zone would they grow in?" asked the President earnestly.

"The Twilight Zone, of course." With that I hung up the phone. That darn Chris.

I now find that the climate in Guantanamo Bay, Cuba, is excellent. The food isn't too bad, considering. I could grow all kinds of houseplants down here if they would let me have anything like that in this cell. Oh, well. It could be worse. At least I don't have to take any more crazy phone calls.

The Great Employee

It was the week before Christmas when a tall man in a dark blue suit and red tie suddenly stepped into the store at Rising Sun Nursery. He stood near the entrance and seemed to survey the layout. With his dark sunglasses and chiseled features, he reminded me of a typical secret service agent. I chuckled. Most of our customers do not wear suits. He was probably just a tourist from the city. He put his finger to his ear, and I realized he was listening to someone. The discreet bulge under his suit now appeared to be a holster. Was this a robbery? Trying not to panic, I slowly eyed the phone and started casually drifting toward it when he stepped toward me.

"Mr. Urbanus? Mr. Don Urbanus?"

"Yes," I said cautiously. "Can I help you with anything?"

"Do you love Christmas, Don? I *can* call you Don?" he asked, staring at me with those glasses so dark, I couldn't see his eyes.

"Sure, sure. Um, yeah, I love Christmas. Who doesn't?"

He looked around briefly and then leaned over confidentially, "You'd be surprised, Don." He stared at me as if trying to decide something.

I chuckled nervously and said, "Do you need—?"

"What I need," he said, interrupting me, "is your help in a matter of grave importance to the world. But I need your word, your *word*, that you won't tell another soul."

Not sure what was going on, I decided to humor him, "You've got it. I won't tell anyone,

Mr . . .?"

"The name's Nick, Jr." He sighed deeply as if a big weight had been lifted from him, and then he put his finger to his ear. "This is Code Green. Santa is coming to town. I repeat, Santa is coming to town." He looked back at me for a moment and then started talking like we were old friends. "Okay, this is the deal, Don. Santa has been kind of depressed lately. Being stuck up at the North Pole, the responsibility and everything, I'm sure you can understand." He paused briefly and looked at me.

"Sure, Nick, sure. I can understand that," I said, nodding my head vigorously.

"Good. Santa needs a break, frankly. He's been hitting the Peppermint Schnapps a little too heavy, if you know what I mean. And then we have Christmas coming up in just a week. I don't think he's ready. He's just not with the Christmas spirit. This is where you come in."

I was tempted to call his bluff. Surely my friend Chris had something to do with this, but then I remembered the time the President called and I hung up on him. I really wasn't ready to visit Cuba again, so I just nodded my head and listened.

"Santa wants a part-time job at your nursery. Don't worry about the paperwork. We have a deal with the IRS. Anyway, he always wanted to work in a retail nursery and be around flowers and stuff. I mean, Don, think of it at the North Pole. The snow. The ice. Pretty boring, don't you think?"

"Oh, I don't know, depends on how cute the girl elves are," I joked. He didn't laugh. I frowned. "Okay, so Santa wants to work here for what, a couple days? A week?"

"I'm hoping just a few hours will do the trick," Nick said, and he nodded toward the parking lot where a very large man with a white beard was being helped out of a van by two men dressed just like Nick. The old man wore huge blue jeans with rolled up cuffs and a big red plaid shirt. He waddled up to me and held out his hand.

"Thank you so much for the opportunity, Don. You don't know how much this means to me."

"No problem," I said, as he firmly gripped my hand. "It's the least I could do, uh . . . 'Joe.'"

With that he peeled off a loud laugh, turning his nose and cheeks cherry red. Then he winked at me and set off toward a customer looking at some of our live Christmas trees. Within minutes, he made a sale. More cars started pulling into the driveway and before we knew it, there was a mad rush for anything to do with Christmas. My employees couldn't keep up with all the customers, so I asked Nick if he could help load the lady in the red pickup and the 'helpers' loaded the man with the blue car. Joe or Santa, or whoever he was, seemed to know the answers to everything! Boy, what an employee! Finally, the last customer waved and smiled, and said, "Merry Christmas." We sat in the store, exhausted, while Judy started counting the checks and cash.

Nick opened the door and leaned in. "Don, we've got to get back now. 'Joe' is feeling much better. I think Christmas is going to come off without a hitch. Thanks. We'll be in touch."

I hopped out of my chair and ran after Nick. "Nick, wait! Do you think Joe would be interested in working in the springtime when we—?" but the van was gone. Everyone was gone. The sun was sinking low, and I caught a gleam off something heading north. Must be an airplane, I thought.

The Bug Blaster

Don's feeble old hands fumbled with the Bug-Blaster™. After sixty years in the nursery business, Don wondered if it was worth trying to keep up with the new ways of doing things. He punched some numbers into the side of the round gadget and then attached a picture of a grasshopper onto a stake. The Bug-Blaster™ hummed to life and shot out of Don's hand. It hovered in the air, rotating, searching for an insect, concluded there were none and went into the rest mode.

"You ding-dong stupid blind piece of worthless junk!" Don wheezed.

He grunted in disgust and grabbed the Bug-Blaster™. Again, numbers were punched and again the blaster malfunctioned. Finally, the blaster managed to identify the grasshopper, but its laser blast was so weak that it didn't even scorch the paper. Don gritted his teeth and turned the laser up to maximum strength. This time the Bug-Blaster zipped out of his hand and efficiently blew a hole right through the paper grasshopper.

"Yes! I knew I could do it! Just takes someone with a little smarts," Don said, pleased with himself. His smile slowly faded as he saw the blaster sputter and fall to the floor. "I'm sorry," said a soothing voice from the blaster. "You have exceeded the safety parameters of this unit. Please contact your local Bug-Blaster™ representative to have this unit reactivated."

"You no good %#**#%*! son of a gun," Don stuttered. He kicked the blaster, and it rolled under a floating chair. "I hate the nursery business. I hate the—"

Don paused in mid-sentence and slowly sat down. His eyes glazed over, and his mind drifted away back to a simpler time. Suddenly he sat up straight and glanced furtively around the room. Quietly he crept over to his old desk and reached underneath for a hidden key. He chuckled softly and rubbed the worn key between his fingers.

Down to the basement he stole. In one corner stood a small plywood cabinet. He patted the cabinet nostalgically. Good old plywood. Now everything was poly-resin somethingorother. Don blew the dust off the rusty lock and stuck the key in. The lock sprang open. He grabbed an illuminator and slowly opened the door.

For a long while he just knelt on the floor and sighed. One by one he took the crusty contents and set them on top of the cabinet. Sevin, Diazonon, Malathion, Roundup, Orthene. All the *good* stuff. He snickered and reached for the bottle of Sevin. There would be some dead grasshoppers tonight.

The Ficus Tree

Don held the door open with his foot, bent down and picked up his Ficus benjamina in the glazed green pot, and walked heavily into the psychiatrist's office. The receptionist, talking quietly on the phone, smiled and pointed at a chair in the corner. Carefully gauging the sturdiness of the coffee table, Don shook his head and set the pot down on the floor. Don chuckled, leaned over and whispered something to the plant.

The receptionist looked over at Don, frowned, and shook her head. Don had been an aspiring nurseryman, the cream of the crop, when something had gone terribly wrong. Now, for the last two years, he had been walking around with an imaginary six-foot-tall Ficus tree named 'Benji'. It was sad. Sadder still was the way Don talked to the tree and seemed to have conversations with it. He was plainly off his rocker. I guess that's the life of a nurseryman, she thought, sane one minute and loonier than a polka-dot petunia the next.

A slightly built lady with frazzled blond hair walked out of the psychiatrist's room and eyed Don, sitting there with a pot and his "friend." Word had gotten around. She paused, glanced at Don and then over at where the plant was supposed to be.

"I don't suppose you have time to answer a gardening question, do you?" Then without waiting for an answer she continued, "I have these Gardenias and they're kind of yellow."

"Not now, Mrs. Thornton," the receptionist said firmly as she eyed Don's face twitch and his blank stare.

"Oh, well," the lady laughed nervously. "Maybe I'll see you at the nursery sometime, or someday?" She looked back at Don and shook her head. She closed the door quietly behind her and left the waiting room.

"You can go in now, Mr. Urbanus. The doctor is waiting."

Don picked up the pot, and with the receptionist holding the door open, he gingerly walked in. Dr. Greenburg looked up from his paperwork, nodded and pointed to the chair.

"Go ahead and sit down, Don. You can put Benji on the table here. It's quite sturdy."

Don quickly got comfortable and lay back on the couch. "I seem to have a problem, Doc. Benji isn't doing so well. He keeps dropping his leaves. Of course, I know that's common with a Ficus benjamina. They don't like to be moved that much. I think it's more serious, though. Benji doesn't seem to like me anymore."

"Really?" said the doctor, still looking down at his notes. "And why do you suppose that is?"

"He says he's tired of moving around and wants to stay in one place."

"And what place might that be?" asked the doctor, slightly smirking.

"He wants to stay right here."

"Here?" The doctor stared sharply at Don. "Why—why would he want to stay here? What do I know about Ficus trees?"

"Benji is getting harder for me to see lately, Doc," Don said, frowning. "It's almost like he's fading away. Do you think I'm getting better, Doc?"

"What do you mean he's fading away?" the doctor said, his voice rising in pitch. "He can't be fading. It's not that easy. You've been one of my most steady patients and believe me when I say that you are *far* from being cured."

"Benji is saying good-bye, Doc. He's disappearing."

"No, he's not disappearing, I tell you. He's as real as this desk."

"I think I'm cured, Doc. I can't see Benji anymore." Don stood up and looked around with wonder.

"I'll tell you when you're cured. Who's the doctor here anyway?" The doctor pointed angrily at the couch. "You just sit back down there. You have another twenty minutes to go."

"I'm cured. You cured me, Doc," Don held up his hands and stared at them. He worked his right hand open and closed as if he was pruning. "I can go back to the nursery business! I can be normal again! Thanks for everything, Doc." Don rushed out of the office and through the waiting room, his hands waving in the air, yelling, "I'm cured. I'm cured" as he ran down the hallway.

The doctor ran after him. "Get back here, you idiot! Get this stupid plant out of my office. I don't want your dumb Ficus tree. Come back here!"

The receptionist went to the door and watched them running down the hallway. She quietly closed the door and sat back down at her desk. She flipped open the schedule book. Ed Swift of Ed's Plant Place was the next client. It was going to be a long day.

What's a Gophicula?

It was a warm autumn day with fall hanging onto summer's tailcoats, refusing to give in to the eventual winter. Halloween was right around the corner but sales at the nursery were still surprisingly good. People were trying to finish some of their outdoor projects while the weather was still nice. I put the phone down as an elderly lady with gray grizzled hair hobbled in with a brown paper bag in one hand and a cane in the other.

"Hello, my name is Mrs. Meyers. I was told I should see the owner. Are you the owner young man?" she asked in a wavering voice.

"I'm Don, the owner. Is there something I can help you with?"

She pursed her lips. "Do you know your stuff? The last nursery I was in didn't have a clue," she said sharply, eyeing me cautiously.

"Why don't you let me see what you have? Maybe I can help." I smiled at her and reached for the bag. She held back and then slowly, reluctantly, handed me the bag. I gazed inside the bag and pulled out what looked like tomato, but it was all white. Also, in the bag was a white carrot with white leaves and a medium-sized zucchini, also white. I frowned and looked over at her.

"You don't know what it is causing this, do you? Nobody does," she challenged me.

"Well," I laughed nervously. "First, I need to ask you a few questions."

"Such as?"

"Are these the only things in your garden that are white like this or are there more? Maybe it is a genetic mutation or a deficiency of some kind," I offered.

"You ninny, my whole garden is like this," she snapped impatiently. "Do you think I would come all this way just to tell you about a white carrot or two?"

I tried to ignore her name-calling and continued with my

questions. "Have you changed your fertilizers or sprayed the plants with anything?"

"Of course not," she sighed. "Can't you see? This was done by an animal. Look at the bite marks on this carrot," she said, pointing with her cane.

I looked carefully at the vegetables and could see a couple of puncture marks on each one. But this was ridiculous. "How did that turn white from an animal?"

"You big dope," she said, getting more and more irritated with me. "I know what did it. I want to know how to kill the darn thing."

Feeling a little lost, I asked her innocently, "Kill what?"

"Why, the gophicula, of course! It's burrowing around and sucking all the green out of my plants."

"What's a gophicula? You mean a gopher did this?" I asked slowly.

"No, you dummy, I said a *gophicula*. Don't they teach you anything at those big fancy schools anymore?"

"Maybe I missed that part. So, what does this gophicula look like, exactly?" I asked.

She held up two fingers as if they were fangs and kind of hissed. I looked at her blankly and scratched my head. I was starting to get a little irritated with this little old lady. First, she was calling me names and then questioning my horticultural knowledge, and finally, coming up with some insane reason for why all these plants were white. I thought I would just give her the old gopher routine about traps and bait and how, with diligence, anyone can rid their yard of even the peskiest gophers.

"And don't go telling me I need traps. I have dozens of traps. You can't kill a gophicula with traps or bait," she said, beating me to the punch.

"Let me get this straight," I paused and rubbed my chin. "This is a sort of gopher with fangs that sucks the color out of all the plants and vegetables and leaves two puncture marks wherever it sucks on the plants. Correct?"

"That's right," she answered, relieved that I was finally catching on.

Obviously, this was some elaborate Halloween joke and my employees had put her up to it. Well, I could play along.

"Well, of course, traps won't work," I said reassuringly. "There is only one thing that will kill a gophicula and that is a wooden stake right through the heart. They hate garlic, of course, but it just discourages them, it won't actually kill them. Since gophers, I mean gophiculas, don't like light, I would suggest trying to kill them at night, when they are active. We happen to sell all kinds of stakes. I suggest a lodge pole, that way you can get it and you won't even have to bend over."

She frowned looking down and then back up at me. "Isn't that dangerous? Couldn't the gophicula . . . I mean, what if he bites me?"

"Nonsense," I said, waving my hand. "Gophiculas are only dangerous to plants. Take it from me, Mrs. Meyers. And after you get rid of your gophiculas, put garlic in the holes and it will keep other gophiculas out."

"Well," she said, finally smiling. "I'm glad I came here. I had my doubts about you, but you certainly make sense. I'll take one stake."

"Do you need some garlic too, Mrs Meyers?" I asked, walking over to the garlic cloves we had for sale.

"Oh, yes, thank you, I almost forgot."

I handed her a pound of garlic and while she was busy, went and got a nice straight lodge pole that I carefully angled over her seats to get it into her car. She thanked me and told me how very helpful I had been. I sent her on her way and wished her luck. As she drove off, I threw her bag of white vegetables in the trash and went out to help another customer. White vegetables! Gophiculas! Give me a break.

I had pretty much forgotten about Mrs. Meyers when she came in suddenly around closing time the day after Halloween. It was getting dark. The time had changed, and it was an hour later than it had been. She had on dark sunglasses and her hand was bandaged, but I noticed she looked different somehow. Her hair appeared to be completely white and her face seemed smoother and more youthful.

"Mrs. Meyers?"

"Oh, Don, I want to thank you for all your help the other day." She grabbed my hand firmly and held on.

I noticed she wasn't carrying her cane and she had on tight black spandex pants. And then I remembered—there was no waver to her voice.

"You *are* Mrs. Meyers?"

"Oh, yes," she said huskily, with her lips slightly parted. "I wasn't feeling quite myself the other day. Now I feel so much better."

"That's nice. No more problems with the gophers, I mean, the gophiculas?" I asked, trying to pull my hand away. Her grip was amazingly strong.

"The what? Oh, no, not at all—in fact, just the opposite. I was just wondering," she sighed helplessly. "You have been such a big help and I would love to have you for dinner." She paused and then said quickly, "You know, to show my appreciation." She stared at me and smiled hungrily.

"I . . . I don't . . . I don't have time for, for that kind of stuff," I said uneasily, yanking my hand out of her grip. I looked around for the other employees. *Where did everyone go? Nobody is ever around when you need them.* "I . . . uh . . . have a lot of work to do at home."

Mrs. Meyers gazed at me critically, her lips in a tight pout, then without a word she turned and walked out of the store. I heaved a big sigh. Some customers can be very strange. Just as suddenly, the employees walked into the store. I felt strangely relieved.

"Are you still here, Don?" asked Denise. "I thought you left."

"No, I was helping that lady," I said. "That Mrs. Meyers."

"What lady? We didn't see any lady." Judy said, as she started counting checks.

"You know that lady," I started to say, "Oh, never mind. By the way, where is George? Did he leave already?"

"George? Oh, he said something about a hot date and a free meal. He just left," Denise answered as she took her phone off her belt and put in on the charger. "Is something wrong?"

I was quiet and thoughtful for a moment. "Judy?" I asked. "You know that garlic you were going to re-order? Why don't you double it? No, triple it. I have a feeling we're going to be selling a lot of garlic pretty soon."

Christmas Eve

It was Christmas Eve. The employees at Rising Sun Nursery had been sent home early, and I was closing the store, anxious to get home. Suddenly I heard a loud humming sound and an eerie light glowed through the sliding door in the breezeway. Alarmed, I walked over to the door and looked out. Immediately, I was immersed in green light and something like a tractor beam seized me and pulled me toward what I assumed was an alien spacecraft. My body was rigid. A door in the ship opened, and I was sucked in.

When I woke up, I found myself strapped to a chair in a large dark room. A green light clicked on and shone on my face. My interrogators were in the shadows.

"You-man," said a high-pitched metallic voice. "We want to ask questions."

"Who are you? Where am I?" I demanded. They ignored me.

"Questions. You answer," it said again. Apparently, they were talking into some electronic translating device because I could hear one of them speaking in a strange gurgling voice to his partner.

"Who are you? What do you want?"

"Tell him who we are," Glorg advised.

Grak glared at Glorg and then reluctantly responded, "Commander Grak am I. This be Glorg."

"Ask him about how they grow plants in those pots," suggested Glorg anxiously. "I want to know how they do it."

"*I* am the one asking questions here," responded Commander Grak importantly. "The High Command of Planet Zerk has other more *strategic* questions they want answered first, Glorg. Just because you are the ship's field biologist doesn't give you the right to ask the first questions."

"All right, all right," Glorg waved a green tentacled hand. "Just remember that we need to get specimens from this planet and they have hundreds of varieties and thousands of specimens here. The scanner is going crazy."

"Yes, yes," sighed Grak. He failed to see the interest in new biological specimens. Why not just attack the planet and wipe out the "you-mans"? Then they could have it all for themselves.

I listened to all this gurgling and slurping with alarm. I got an uncomfortable feeling, like maybe they were going to eat me. The first alien spoke into the device again.

"You-man. Who is Santa Claus?"

I sat staring at them. "Santa Claus?"

Glorg frowned. "Maybe he didn't understand. Ask again."

"You-man. Who is Santa Claus?"

"You want to know who Santa Claus is?" I asked, dumfounded.

"Hmm. Maybe this you-man is not very smart," stated Grak, "This is the third time he has answered with a question."

"You're not doing it right. Let me try." Glorg grabbed the translator. Grak glared at him.

"You-man. Tell us—"

"First of all, my name is Don, not you-man," I answered angrily. "Secondly, Santa is this guy that deliveries toys to children all over the world in one night. And that would be tonight."

"See?" smiled Glorg, "You just have to know how to ask."

Grak rolled his large eye and sighed, or rather gurgled.

"Morning, we want to know where this Santa lives?" asked Glorg.

"It's not dawn or morning. The name is Don, got it? And Santa is supposed to live at the North Pole, although nobody knows where exactly." *What was this all about? Why were they asking me about a mythical person? What was I doing here? I still had presents to wrap.*

Glorg glanced over at Grak and smiled feebly. "It's kind of touchy, but at least it is talking."

Grak sighed heavily. "I guess our information was correct about the North Pole although our scanners have not been able to locate this Santa. He must have very advanced cloaking devices to hide from us. Think of the speed of his ship if he is able to go all around the world and deliver gifts to—wait a second." Grak looked at his communicator. "How many young you-mans are there on this planet?"

"Over a billion," answered Glorg glumly. "Think of his production and delivery capabilities. A billion units delivered in one night? Unheard of."

"I don't see how we can chance an attack on this planet. It is just too risky. This Santa Claus sounds like a very formidable foe." Grak tapped his tentacles together thoughtfully. "I suggest we report back immediately to the High Command."

"What about the you-man? And what about my biological samples you promised?" Glorg demanded.

"Oh, very well. Dump this you-man out and get whatever samples you need, but hurry up. If I'm late again for X-mss, my wife will kill me. My kids will kill me," gurgled Grak, more forcefully.

"I know," smiled Glorg, "I was late getting in last X-mss Eve and my son thought I was the giant Blorg delivering treats to all the good little Zerkians."

Concerned, I listened to their strange gurgling. It seemed like they were coming to a decision about something. Was I going to be Christmas dinner on some alien planet? Suddenly I was unceremoniously forced out the ship's door and deposited on the ground. The ship zoomed up over the nursery. A green light shone down and sucked up half the one-gallon section, then in a blink, the ship disappeared into the darkening sky.

I stood there a minute and thought about what had just happened. Somehow, I felt as if I had done something important but wasn't exactly sure what. How was I going to explain the missing plants? But it was late, and I had promised my daughter that we would sing Christmas carols and watch *How the Grinch Stole Christmas*. And maybe, if she was good, she could open one present from us. The rest of her presents, of course, would be delivered after midnight by you-know-who.

The Hungry Customers

Zorg and Zak, two pale green aliens from the planet Zuton, looked down on the western United States from their spaceship in orbit. Zorg fumbled with his new Google Earth app trying to make sense of it all.

"Never mind the app," complained Zak. "Don't you have a guide on places to eat? Look up that."

"I would if I knew where we were," snapped Zorg.

"What about that place—Kaleefornya?" asked Zak, pointing a wispy green tendril at a point on the map. Just then his stomach gurgled and groaned in protest. He sighed. He was so sick of eating creamed vegetables out of tubes. Surely a little visit to the planet couldn't hurt, could it?

"Wait! Here's a place. It's called Star Bucks. Maybe they have food for interstellar travelers?" Zorg looked up hopefully.

"More likely a money exchange station. I wonder what the exchange rate is on zutons for dollars?"

"We'll just make sure we stay away from any big cities. No sense attracting too much attention. Say, here's a little town called Valley Springs. I'll just dial in the coordinates."

"Sounds good to me," said Zak, pointing the craft down toward the planet. "Anything will be better than that paste."

At about a thousand feet off the ground, the ship leveled off as Zorg peered down, trying to find the Starbucks. "There it is. Hey, cool, they have a drive-up window!"

Zak zoomed silently down and patiently waited behind a car. The driver was reaching for a large cappuccino from the cashier when, looking behind him, suddenly dropped it. The top popped off, and the creamy liquid oozed out onto the asphalt. The driver gunned the engine and peeled off in a blaze of burnt rubber. The cashier peered out the drive-in window at the fleeing car, shaking her head.

"Bummer," said Zak. "He dropped his cup." He silently glided forward and opened the hatch, eager to place his order.

"Good morning. What can I . . . ?"

Zak gave his most charming smile, showing numerous rows of sharp black teeth, and made a circle with his green tendril—a symbol of friendship on Zuton. The cashier's eyes went wide, and her mouth hung open stupidly. Suddenly she let loose an ear-piercing scream and stumbled away, clawing at the air. Zak slammed the hatch, zoomed up a few thousand feet, and then leveled off.

"Man, I forgot the stupid disguises."

Zorg looked down again. "Wait a second. There's a green patch down there. Maybe they have some food we could eat? Let me look at the app. Oh, that location is called Rising Sun Nursery. What do you suppose that means? Is it a bakery? Maybe they make bread."

"I don't know, and I don't care," answered Zak. "As long as they have something we can eat. Hmm. They seem to have hundreds of green things in containers. Take-n-bake? Go get the disguises. I'll park the ship behind that hill and we'll just walk over to the store."

Zorg quickly pulled out two trench coats, two wide-brimmed hats, sunglasses, masks, and gloves while Zak quietly parked the ship in the back field of the nursery. They looked at each other as they assembled their disguise. Satisfied, they opened the hatch and climbed out.

Don had just finished helping three customers. One had a wilted leaf to show him and wanted to know what it was. Another one wanted to know if her husband had killed their almond tree after he had painted the entire trunk and branches with tar. And the last one wanted to know if rooting hormone would help a graft heal quicker. He turned around to see two short customers wearing trench coats and dark sunglasses. One held a pale-green sickly vine of some sort in his gloved hand. Don grabbed it and looked closely. It was slightly dry and sticky. It obviously needed water and some nutrients whatever it was.

"You idiot," Zak whispered. "Your tendril is showing."

"I know that now," answered Zorg, glaring at Zak as Don examined him.

To Don, it sounded like a strange foreign language, so he did what every person does to someone who doesn't understand English. He talked slowly and loudly. "It looks like you need more water for your plant. You know, water?"

"Why is he yelling at me?" asked Zorg.

"Maybe he is trying to tell us about food. He looks very concerned about your tendril. Now that I think about it, you do look a little pale," Zak said, nodding his head as he looked at Don.

Sensing that the one moving his head understood, Don started talking to him. "You need to water every day when it gets hot in the summer. Water . . . every . . . day," Don repeated slowly, pointing at Zorg's tendril, and making a motion as if he was drinking water. Zak nodded again.

"What did he say?" asked Zorg.

Zak frowned as he listened. "I don't have a clue. I think he's talking about food, though."

Don waved for them to follow. They shuffled into the store and glanced around at the high ceiling and numerous shelves of gifts.

"Cool store," whispered Zorg, looking at the puppets with interest. He noticed a snail puppet and shuddered. He never wanted a run-in with those militant flesh eaters again.

Don showed them the Best Fertilizer Pills on the counter and picked one up. "You also need to fertilize. You know, fertilize?"

Zak held up his gloved hands showing ten fingers.

"You have ten plants?" Don asked.

Zak nodded.

"What sizes are the plants?"

Zorg held up the glove that didn't have his tendril showing.

"It's a five-gallon size? Well then, you need three fertilizer tabs per plant. So, you need thirty tablets." Don grabbed a bag and started filling it with tablets.

"Oh boy, oh boy," said Zak, holding out his hands for the bag, Don handed it to him and walked around to the register to ring them up.

"You did bring some money, didn't you?" asked Zak, glancing over at Zorg.

"Me? I thought *you* brought it."

They both looked at Don.

"Run for it!" yelled Zak as he dashed out the door. Startled, Zorg ran after Zak, losing his hat as he ran through the doorway.

"Hey," yelled Don. "Come back here!" By the time he got around the counter and out the door, Zak and Zorg were already headed over the hill, running amazingly fast for two short people. As Don got to the top of the rise, he saw a flash of light. There was nothing there but an empty field. Whoever they were, they were long gone. He went back to the store and picked up the hat. Nice hat, he thought, noticing the unusual weave. He put it on his head. It fit.

Already far out into space and heading away from earth, Zak opened the bag and popped a fertilizer tab into his mouth and sighed contentedly. "Man," he said, handing the bag to Zorg. "What we have to go through to get some decent food around here."

The Garden of Eden

Installed a sign after a suggestion by an employee. It was an offhand comment, but looking at the sign now, it seemed very appropriate. I smiled as I looked at my handiwork. As I was walking back to the office, a bright young couple approached me. She had long light-brown hair and he was an average-sized good-looking fellow.

"Can you help us?" she asked. "I understand that you're the owner of Rising Sun Nursery, and we have a lot of questions about fruit trees and such."

"Eve, he's probably busy. I am sure we can figure this out on our own."

"Really, Adam, he's the expert. Why not get his opinion?"

"That's okay," I assured him. "I can help you. What exactly are you looking for?"

"Well—" he began, but Eve interrupted him.

"We want every kind of fruit," she said enthusiastically. "I am *especially* fond of apples."

"Apples?" he complained. "We already have an apple tree in our garden and we never get any fruit off that thing. I want peaches and apricots and stuff like that."

"Adam," she said patiently, as if talking to a child, while nervously fingering her necklace, "I happen to like apples the best. You should try apples some time. They're better than any other fruit as far as I'm concerned. You can eat them fresh or make pies and applesauce out of them. All kinds of things."

"I don't like apples," he said stubbornly.

"We have quite a variety of apples," I explained, as I led them down to our 5-gallon fruit tree section. "There are sweet ones and tart ones for cooking, and everything in between." I noticed her necklace was an unusual design of a snake. "Interesting necklace," I noted.

"Do you like it? I love it. I wear it everywhere. I just love snakes for some reason." She gazed admiringly at her necklace.

"I hate snakes. Anyway, why do we always have to start talking about snakes?" Adam complained. "I thought we were here to get some fruit trees."

"How come we don't get any apples on the tree we have?" she asked me abruptly.

"Well, there could be lots of reasons. Sometimes it's the weather, or perhaps they are not getting pollinated by bees. If you have only one apple tree, you might need a pollinizer."

"A pollinizer? What's that?" she asked, intensely interested.

"Who cares?" Adam sighed. He began wandering away, looking at the nametags on the rows of fruit trees.

"Some apple trees need another apple tree to pollinize them because they are self-sterile. Do you know what kind of apple you have?" I asked.

"No," she said, frowning. "But it's very old. It was there long before we bought our place."

"Well you might get a couple of apple trees, then. That way they will be sure to pollinize each other and the old apple tree, too."

She smiled radiantly. "That's a wonderful idea! Maybe we can finally get some apples on that old tree. You'll see, dear," she called over to Adam. "When you get a taste of a really good apple, it will probably change your life." She smiled and winked at me. "I will get him to eat an apple. You'll see."

"I like things just the way they are," he grumbled back at us.

"By the way," she said, fingering her necklace again. "Love your sign. 'The Garden of Eden.' Very clever."

"Thanks," I said. "If you need any more help, let me know."

"Oh," she said. "I think I can handle things here." She walked away gracefully, her long hair swaying with each step.

The Leafist

Don had been a successful retail nurseryman but had given it all up for his real passion as a Leafist. He carefully adjusted the turban on his head, smoothed his green robe, and stepped outside his colorful signature booth—a canopy covered with pictures of leaves.

The county fair was a pretty good gig. Still, he was hoping for more and larger venues where he could demonstrate his unique abilities and satisfy the cravings for adulation that fed his ego. Perhaps on *Oprah* or *The Late Show?* It was just a matter of time.

He glared at another canopy set up not more than twenty feet from his own. It was one of those 'run-of-the-mill' palmists seen at every Renaissance Faire. "Madame Hugo" was painted in gaudy pink letters on a sign hanging outside her booth. *Madame Hugo? What kind of a name was that?* Don snorted, and went back inside his canopy to arrange the chairs where his customers would sit eagerly awaiting his every word. He arranged his own sign with tastefully carved green letters spelling "Dr. Don" and he set his business cards carefully off to one side of the table. Of course, he wasn't a 'doctor' in the literal sense, it was more of a nickname, but he had paid his dues over many years. He had earned it. Besides, it had a certain ring to it.

Don had been studying leaves ever since he was a child. He was always fascinated by them, especially tree leaves. He estimated he must have read at least fifty thousand leaves in his long-storied career. Now at the pinnacle of his insight and powers, he hit the road to show the world what he knew. He glanced outside his canopy and smiled. A middle-aged lady carrying a plastic bag was hurrying toward his booth.

"Oh, Dr. Don! I am so glad you are here. I used to go to my local nursery, but they got squeezed out by all those big box stores."

"Well," said Dr. Don, placing a finger and thumb on his chin thoughtfully. "Why don't you go to them for advice?"

She rolled her eyes. "Oh, really, Dr. Don."

Don smirked. "Well, what do you have for me, Miss?"

"Oh, it's Sheila." She smiled and pulled some leaves out of her plastic bag. The leaves were fresh and supple—unlike the dried and crispy leaves that some customers brought in. He felt a kinship with her already.

He chose the first leaf and smiled slightly. Years of nursery work had made this an easy pick, but he played his part. He frowned and turned the leaf around, studying it carefully. "It's palmate in shape, which generally suggests a northern climate."

"Oh, yes. I knew that." She bit her lip and leaned forward eagerly.

"The size and texture suggest an oriental background. This is a Japanese maple leaf," he stated firmly.

"Excellent!" she clapped her hands together. "I thought it might be something like that."

"The size and color of the leaf suggests that it most likely is a potted tree that is probably root bound and without sufficient nutrients. Notice the slight stress lines on the outside ridge of the leaf? You should protect it from the afternoon sun, re-pot it with fresh soil or put it in a larger container and give it some slow release fertilizer at least twice a year in the spring and summer."

Her jaw dropped open in amazement. "That is amazing! I don't know how you do it." She grabbed her checkbook and scribbled out a check still shaking her head. "I don't know what we would do without you traveling Leafists."

Don clasped his hands and shrugged slightly. *What indeed?* He thanked Sheila who kept bubbling over about all her friends she was going to send to him. *Yes, this is what it was all about. Servicing the world one leaf at a time—and getting paid for it.* He placed the check in a small metal box and put it back under his chair. He turned around and was startled to see a woman standing there in the entryway. This, obviously, was Madame Hugo.

She stood there, hands on hips, with loose flowing lavender pants and a pink long-sleeved top. Her large, dark blue eyes, heavy with eyeliner, stared down at him, taking him in—his canopy and everything inside it—with one swift decisive glance.

"I have some leaves I want you to identify." It was not a request but a challenge.

Don motioned with his hand to the chair, and his eyes locked onto hers.

"Come sit down."

She entered slowly, sat down gracefully, and produced a bag of leaves somewhere from the folds of her pants.

"Why are you—?" Don started.

"Called Madame Hugo? It seems more mysterious." She offered no more, and Don asked no more. She pulled out a leaf and slapped it down on the table.

Don glanced at it briefly and stared back at her. "A pinnately compound leaf. The leaflets are shorter than some of their species. Coloring and shape suggests a Raywood ash."

She slapped down another leaf. "You can use Latin if you wish. And don't bother with the descriptions."

He took the leaf and put it up to his nose just to be sure. "*Cinnamomum camphora.*"

She slapped down another leaf.

"*Betula pendula.*"

She continued to place one leaf after another on the table.

"*Salix integra Hakura Nishiki, Lauris nobilis. Eucalyptus polyanthemus. Albizia julibrissin.*"

She glared at Don and then a tiny smile creased her lips. She set the last leaf down on the table. Don reached for the leaf and turned it over carefully to catch the light. It was familiar. He had seen it before, but it had been over thirty years.

"Well?" she demanded.

Don took a deep breath, searching his mind. She rose up, almost crouching over him like a cat stalking a mouse. Don shut his eyes, following the path back to his memories. The only sound was her breathing, and he blocked that out of his mind.

"*Lyonothamnus floribundus asplenifolius.*"

"Ahhh," she sputtered in frustration. "Very well, I will admit that you are very accomplished at what you do."

"And you?" Don asked, holding out his palm. She sat back down, took his hand and caressed it open, looking at every fingerprint, every crease. She took his other hand and studied it equally, absorbing every line, every contour. One eyebrow lifted slightly and then she turned her dark eyes onto his.

"Dr. Don, there you are! Oh, are you busy? We can wait." Two heavy-set middle-aged women backed out of the booth.

"No, I am just leaving. Just give me a moment." She glanced back at Don. "Come to my tent after the fair closes. I will tell you your life purpose and life lessons that may be holding you back from achieving that which you want the most." She turned without another word and walked quickly out of the booth.

"Oh, good! Now, we have lots of leaves we want you to look at. Jeannie, get your other bag out," insisted the taller of the two.

Don walked past the two women and glanced out of the canopy, but Madame Hugo was already out of sight. Don raised his hands and looked at each one. My life purpose, he thought, what was she talking about?

"Oh, Dr. Don. Are you going to read our leaves?" asked the shorter lady. "I especially want you to look at my sister-in-law's cousin's leaf. They don't know *what's* wrong with it."

"Um, yes, yes." He walked thoughtfully around the table, sat down and smiled. "Now, how can I help you lovely ladies?"

They chatted happily away, but Don's mind was distracted. *Could palms be read like leaves?* He decided he would take Madame Hugo up on her offer.

"That's an Azalea and this one is a Gardenia. Looks like the variety Mystery because of the size. They both need some iron," he mumbled absentmindedly.

The two women broke out in smiles and looked at each other. In unison they declared, "That's amazing!"

After they left, Don was irritated. How could Madame Hugo

tell him what *his* life purpose was? He *knew* his life purpose. Didn't he? He was doing it, wasn't he? He adjusted his turban and sat down waiting for the next customer. Except the rest of the afternoon, no one came to his tent. Even more irritating, there was a line outside Madame Hugo's tent. He gritted his teeth.

The crowds thinned as closing time approached. As soon as the fair closed, he marched over to her tent, not bothering to take off his robe and turban. Madame Hugo was sitting there in worn jeans and a blue T-shirt, drinking a glass of red wine. Her blond hair, probably dyed, Don thought savagely, was loose on her shoulders.

"You want a glass of wine? You like merlot?"

Don was taken aback. "Um, sure, I suppose."

She got a glass and slowly filled it half-full and handed it to him.

"You think you're pretty observant, right?"

"Sure. Yeah. I think I am."

She scoffed. "But you don't recognize me?"

"Recognize you?" I stared at her for a while, my mind racing.

"Have I changed that much since college?"

"Mary? The tool girl at the Horticulture Unit?"

"Very good," she smiled. "You, on the other hand, I recognized in an instant, even with that ridiculous getup on." She laughed, and I smiled.

"You look fantastic! It took me a long time to get over you. I heard you married. He died?"

"No, divorce. I should have married you. I've been trying to find you. I heard you were single again."

"So, this whole thing? It's a sham? You don't read palms?"

She stood up. "Oh no. I read palms. Give me yours."

I held out my hand, she took it, pulled me close, and placed it on her waist. She tossed my turban aside and wrapped her arms around my neck. She pulled me even closer and kissed me passionately. I responded gladly. After several minutes, we parted breathlessly.

"Come with me. Give up this traveling Leafist thing. We were meant to be together."

"But it is my destiny to be a Leafist. It's my calling. I could never give it up. It's my whole life's purpose. I would be empty without it. I just can't do it."

"I won the lottery. My name is Mary Peters now. You know, it was all in the news."

"You're the one who won the $300 million jackpot?"

"Yes."

She looked up into his eyes with passion and yearning. The years peeled away. It was as if they were young again. Just then, one of the groundskeepers entered the tent.

"Oh, Dr. Don, there you are. I have a leaf of a tree that I've been wondering . . . Dr. Don?" The groundskeeper slowly exited the tent. Dr. Don was occupied with something other than leaves. He had a new life's purpose.

The Green Vote

Senator Green sat alone in his Washington office, stroking the stubble on his chin and clutching yesterday's newspaper. Members of his own party were calling for him to abandon his quest for the presidency. He sighed and glanced at yesterday's headline splashed across *The New York Times*: "Green Talks to Plants." The article continued with vague accusations questioning the senator's sanity and quotes from colleagues who were "shocked and saddened" to hear of his sudden fall from grace.

His whole idea of trying to connect with the common people had backfired. His aides, his chief of staff, his campaign manager had all warned him he was making a terrible mistake. They said he was too stiff and lacked emotion. How better to connect with people then to show them his personal side? Anyway, he rose to the stature of a presidential candidate by going with his gut feeling. He wasn't going to change now. What a mess he made.

It all started when that irritating reporter from *The Times*, Linda Lockwood, requested a personal interview with him at his home. The TV camera was rolling, the lights were on, what was he supposed to do? His campaign manager made a slashing motion across his throat, but he ignored him and agreed to the interview.

It started inauspiciously when Linda stumbled in his greenhouse, broke her heel, and got a handful of green algae when she reached out to catch herself. The rest of the interview she bobbed up and down, following him past his prized collection of orchids. He was particularly proud of his fragrant Cattleyas and the arching sprays of Phalaenopsis. He had even started dabbling in tuberous begonias. It was all lost on Linda, who, in her garish outfit and drenched in perfume, couldn't see the difference between a Cymbidium and an Oncidium.

He wandered through the greenhouse talking to 'his little beauties', praising one and consoling another that looked a little pale. Linda immediately pounced on that fact. She grilled him on it, completely ignoring the finer points of orchid propagation.

"Linda," he responded casually. "People talk to their cats and dogs. They talk to their Guinea pigs and parakeets. Why shouldn't I talk to my plants? I like talking to plants."

Unfortunately, Linda only quoted the last sentence in her article and concluded that maybe it wasn't such a good idea to have the most powerful man in the world, the man with his finger on the nuclear button, wandering around babbling to inanimate objects. Yes, he had sadly miscalculated and now his dream, his ambition to be president, was gone like a coleus in a hard frost.

There was a commotion outside his office door, and suddenly his campaign manager burst into the room and slammed the door behind him, cutting off a few reporters waving cameras.

"There you are, Senator. Where have you been? I've been looking all over for you."

"Just waiting for the funeral, Jim," the senator heaved a sigh. "They can bury me and plant a tree on top."

"What are you talking about? Haven't you seen today's paper or been watching the TV?" Jim asked, incredulously.

"What's the point?" scoffed the senator, tossing the newspaper in the direction of his manager. "We're finished."

"Senator, Linda Lockwood was exposed as a paid operative of your opponent hired to do a hit piece on you. Every garden club in America is ready to support your candidacy now. Hell, every gardener will support you now. Even the pet owners are on your side. The phone calls and emails are streaming in. It's something I never calculated on, sir. The gardener vote! We can call it the 'Green Vote'. After all, gardening is the number one hobby in America. Why didn't I think of that? Senator, you are a genius! I can see it now," Jim said, framing his hands in a square. "A plant in every pot, and a 'Green' house in every backyard."

Jim looked back at the senator and suddenly noticed his rumpled appearance. "Senator, you have to get ready for a news conference. I have you scheduled for one in an hour. Well, what are you waiting for? Go get cleaned up. It's on to the White House!"

The senator stood up straight and tall. He was ready to take on the world. His dream was again within his grasp and all because of his love of plants. *Amazing!* he mused. *It's a good thing that I didn't mention that the plants talk back.*

The Tree Sale

The tree sale at Rising Sun Nursery was over. The crowds were gone. Don plodded over to close the gate. It had been a long but satisfying weekend.

A few customers, suspicious about the blowout prices, asked if there was something wrong with the trees. No, Don had joked, they just need homes. It was time to move them out and get them in the ground. You can't hang on to these trees forever, he had said. As he swung the gate shut, he noticed a few trees still hanging onto the fence.

"Hey," Don yelled over at them. "I thought I told you guys to beat it. Nobody wanted you. Either scram, or it's the compost pile for you."

"But y'all promised us homes," complained a southern magnolia. "Where are we all gonna go? Who's gonna take care of us?"

"I never made any promises," Don snapped. "Besides, it was just an advertisement, okay? 'Don't let our trees go homeless,' it said. Hey, this isn't a cradle to grave establishment here. You washed out, so you're on your own."

"But I'll be homeless as well as fruitless," complained a fruitless mulberry.

"Too bad." Don grabbed some of the trees and began setting them outside the gate. He grabbed a smoke tree by its trunk.

"Wait a minute. I have a question."

"What is it?" Don asked impatiently.

"Got any cigarettes?"

"No! Any other stupid questions?" Don shoved the smoke tree outside the gate. He walked over to the weeping willow and braced for what was to come. The willow burst into tears with big jerky sobs wracking it and shaking its leaves. Don brushed off the water and set the tree outside.

"You . . . you raised me from a cutting. I remember when you cut me and put me in the greenhouse and rooted me. I remember when my roots first felt the soil. And I grew and grew. I did it for you," the willow said, choked with emotion.

"Yeah, well, you grew too fast. Look at you. You're root bound." He grabbed the flowering dogwood and noticed that his pant leg was all wet. "Darn it!"

Out went a cork oak, a silver dollar gum, a coast redwood, a dwarf mugho pine, a Colorado blue spruce, and a prickly pear cactus.

"Look, all of you. I just don't have room for you anymore. I don't know if you noticed, but there are a lot of younger trees growing in the nursery. Maybe you'll get lucky and someone will come along and pick you up." Don set out a sign facing the highway, closed and locked the gate, and walked away. He didn't want to think about them anymore. It wasn't his fault. He had done his best.

"Well," the spruce said philosophically. "I guess we had best make the best of it. I, myself, am going to try to get spruced up a bit in case someone comes along."

"That's easy for you to say," quipped the cork oak. "You're a spruce. Anyway, with so many wineries around here, I am likely to get taken before any of you."

The coast redwood snickered. "Cork is on the way out, Corky. Everyone is going to plastic. Anyway, I will be around long after all of you are compost."

The cactus was very distressed. "Come on everyone, we need to stick together here."

"Y'all got a point there," agreed the southern magnolia. Nobody else seemed much inclined, however, to take the cactus up on his suggestion. An Elberta peach tree in the back quietly hung a sign from a branch that said, 'Will grow food for water', and shuffled away from them and closer to the street.

"We just need to take care of ourselves," explained the silver dollar gum. "Why, with a little money, we can—"

"Where are *you* going to get money?" sneered the dwarf mugho pine. "Money doesn't grow on trees."

"Oh, you don't think I can, Shorty?"

"Yeah, sure, pick on the one tree that is vertically challenged. Big tough guy, aren't you?" the pine said, puffing out his stubby branches.

Suddenly, the Japanese maple was among them. Her palmate leaves unfolded slowly, and she looked up at them as if just awakening from a deep meditative state. They stared at her, transfixed, unbelieving that a valuable tree like her was being abandoned by the man. What was she doing here? And yet, here she was, calm, at peace, grounding them, giving them encouragement like a dose of refreshing water.

"Be at peace," she began. "We need man, but man needs us."

"Not that man," sniffed the weeping willow.

"But *some* man," replied the maple. "We need only use the forces of the Law of Attraction and someone will come. We are *free* trees. By using the forces of nature, we can attract the right person to come to us."

"But how?" asked the oak.

"By deep concentration and meditation on what you desire," the maple said, and immediately closed its leaves and started chanting. The other trees looked around at each other, shrugged, and began an unharmonious racket that sounded a lot like leaves scraping together. The willow, never one to bend to new fads, and taller than the other trees, noticed a pickup truck driving down the highway past the nursery.

"The hell with that chanting stuff," he mumbled, spread his branches out to the maximum and let the wind slowly topple him over. He crashed on the pavement. All the trees immediately stopped chanting. Even the Japanese maple blinked and looked around.

George and Myrna were driving down the highway past the nursery in their old Chevy pickup when Myrna saw some movement out of the corner of her eye.

"George, quick, pull into the nursery parking lot."

George, used to Myrna's instant instructions on their weekend jaunts to garage sales, immediately turned and roared up the driveway. They both got out and looked at the sign next to the trees.

"It says 'Free to a Good Home.' I expect they meant us, don't you think, Myrna?"

The weeping willow looked up with a start. "What did the sign say?"

Myrna noticed the tree sprawled on the ground. "Oh, look! A weeping willow! I always wanted a weeping willow, George!"

George glanced at the assortment of trees. "A peach tree, a mulberry, look—even a silver dollar tree! We can grow our own money, Myrna. Maybe now I can get you that ring I've been promising you."

"Oh, George," Myrna giggled, as she helped him load the trees onto the bed of the pickup. "Should we leave any for anyone else?"

"It says to a good home. I don't know any home better'n ours."

The Japanese maple peered back toward the office. She could swear she saw someone peeking out the window. She nodded knowingly, and then she too was loaded into the pickup. They got in, laughed, and drove down the driveway and onto the highway. When they were gone, Don came out, unlocked the gate, and walked out to the sign. He glanced at the words, 'Free to Good Home,' smiled, and carried the sign back inside the nursery.

Astrology for Plants

Don needed a new gimmick. The sales at Rising Sun Nursery were flat. There had to be some way to generate some excitement. He sighed, sat down, and opened the local paper to the Horoscope section and glanced at Taurus. "Pay attention to family. Someone admires you from afar. It's time to finish that project you were putting off."

"Yeah, right," he muttered. "I could write this stuff and do a better job. Instead of people, I could write about plants. I could—" He stared blankly, his mind abuzz. He stood up and walked across the store as if in a trance.

Susan was stocking a shelf as Don passed by. "Uh oh," Susan whispered to Denise. "He's got that look."

"That usually means more work for us," sighed Denise, closing the cash register drawer.

By the end of the week, Don had built a small enclosure in a corner of the warehouse and curtained it off with a lavender cloth drape. Little silver moons and stars sprinkled the cloth. Don's eyes wandered around and locked onto a Bistro set for sale. He grabbed the small round table and placed it inside with the two chairs on either side. "Ah, the sign!" Don said to nobody as he marched outside.

Susan sneaked into the warehouse to see what was going on. Don had been very secretive and if there was one thing Susan hated, it was a secret she didn't know. She took the whole scene in at a glance and then took a picture with her cell phone. She spun around and headed out the door when Don walked right into her, carrying a large white sign.

"Oh, Susan, here, give me a hand with this, okay? I need you to hold this sign for me while I screw it onto the wall here."

Don walked away to get the screw gun, leaving Susan holding the sign. She peeked at the word 'Hortiscopes' in large black letters blazed across the top of the sign with smaller green words below spelling 'for every plant.' Don came back with the screw gun.

"Hortiscopes?" Susan asked. "What's that?"

"You've heard of horoscopes, right? Well, this is horoscopes, except it's for plants. Hortiscopes. Got it?" Don smiled and started screwing the sign up.

Susan frowned, wondering if Don had been playing in the fertilizer a little too much.

An elderly lady with a plastic bag wandered in. "Excuse me. Are you Don? I understand you can tell me what this plant is and how to take care of it." She held up the bag and Don took it.

"Please, come back to my chamber and have a seat."

Susan ran back into the store and grabbed Denise. "You've got to come and listen to this. Don's in his 'chamber' and he's talking to some lady."

Denise glanced around. There were no customers close by. "Okay. Let's go." They both hurried back to listen.

". . . and the Ginkgo is known as an elder plant because of the age of this species. It has been around for many millions of years and has a high spiritual energy. It is ruled by the planet Saturn because of its long life. The fruit or nuts are dried and used as a male fertility symbol."

"I had no idea," the elderly lady said, looking closely at the leaves. "I thought it was an unusual tree. I can see I need to treat it with more respect."

"Definitely with respect," Don repeated. "This tree has often been grown near temples in China. In fact, that is probably how it survived. It is sometimes called the tree of life."

"My goodness," the lady said. "But what about the future of this tree? It seems to be struggling a bit. What should I do?"

"Well, since Neptune will soon be in conjunctivitis with Juniper, the spiritual energy of the tree will be highest in about three days. I would say that now is a good time to fertilize and mulch it."

"Amazing that you can read all of that from one little leaf. You can be sure that I will tell all my friends. Now, point me in the direction of the best fertilizer and mulch you have," the lady stated, standing up.

Denise turned and looked at Susan. Susan looked back and shrugged. They quickly left and went back to the store.

"But now is the time to fertilize anyway," Denise argued.

"I know that. You know that. And Don knows—" Susan whispered, but cut it short as Don walked in. They watched him silently as he walked across the store. He seemed to be lost in thought again.

"Hmm," Don muttered, rubbing his chin. "I wonder who admires me from afar?"

A Most Impressive Establishment

Warden Green pulled up to the entrance gate, leaned out of the car, and showed his authorization pass. Sitting next to him was Senator Blade, the powerful Chairman of the Senate Committee on Appropriations. A heavily armed guard, blocking the way, signaled to the tower to open the gate.

"Go right on in, sir."

The huge gate slowly creaked open. Once inside, two guards on electric scooters motioned to follow them. The warden turned to Senator Blade and gave a quick nod of assurance. The senator glanced doubtfully out the window.

"Is this place secure, Green?"

"Oh, yes, sir, Senator. Notice the guard towers every hundred feet, the twenty-foot-high wall laced with rolls of razor wire, and the men have been trained in the latest high-tech weaponry for any unexpected outbreaks."

The senator grunted. "Well, you do seem to have a lot of guards on duty. I guess you could call it a growth industry, eh Green? Keeps the little people busy, I suppose."

"Yes, sir," the warden nodded in approval. "And jobs mean more votes. Right, Senator?"

Before the senator could respond, a siren cut the air, and half a dozen guards wearing backpack sprayers poured out of a nearby building.

"A show for my benefit?" the senator asked skeptically.

The men raced over to where a small weed poked out along the fence. They sprayed it unmercifully with Round-Up and then added a good dose of pre-emergent all around the area. As quickly as it started, the emergency was over. The men marched back to their building at a fast trot.

"Most impressive," mumbled the senator, rubbing his chin.

"I told you, sir. Using extra prison guards in the nursery business was a true stroke of genius. As you can see, the taxpayer's money is certainly not being wasted. No illegal alien weeds or bugs are going to infiltrate *this* nursery!"

"Yes," agreed the senator, nodding his head slowly. "This nursery, what is it called?"

"Rising Sun Nursery, sir."

"Yes, it is a most impressive establishment."

The Great Decline

I had been in the business of *selling* plants at Rising Sun Nursery, but that was before the "Great Decline" as the world now calls the depletion of the earth's oxygen. Plants that I sold for six bucks could now be sold for hundreds or even thousands of dollars, but I wasn't about to sell them for any price. My family needed all the oxygen our nursery produced, and, because we were in an oxygen-producing industry, the government gave us extra coupons for air canisters.

It all started only six months before when an unscrupulous lab assistant had seen Cindy Crawford at a local restaurant, got some of her hair that had fallen on the floor (probably because she kept tossing her head around so much). He cloned her DNA on a dare by the janitor and injected her genetic material into his wife's rather rotund body.

Things began to happen instantly. His wife quickly changed into a ravishing beauty, left the lab assistant and his lowly salary, and ran off with the janitor who had just won the lottery. In a fit of despair, the lab assistant threw the bottle of DNA into the ocean and went back to his job. Unfortunately, the cap of the bottle was cork and became dislodged in the pounding California surf, thus changing our world forever.

The first reports came in from sport fishermen noticing that the fish they were catching all had strange moles on the left side of their mouths. Panic quickly ensued when small scaly bodies washed up on the beaches, all looking like little Cindy Crawford's. Scientists had more grim news. Not only animals, but algae and plankton were also changing into mini-Cindy's. There was a massive die-off as the ocean's ecosystem collapsed.

No one even thought about the consequences of this collapse until, during a long speech by the president in the east wing of the newly dedicated Virginia Slims Medical Clinic, he suddenly fainted and had to be revived by an emphysema patient carrying a portable oxygen tank. A shock wave of realization rippled around the world as scientists slapped their foreheads simultaneously. Of course! The ocean produces 80 percent of the world's oxygen! At man's present consumption rate, the world had only eight months of oxygen left, at least to sustain life, excluding cockroaches of course.

There was a sudden surge of interest in gardening and all the people who had previously just been romanticizing about working at a nursery, now began to pester me day after day about a job or even just to help at no pay. At first, all the books about growing plants were sold. Then all the seeds. Then began a feverish buying spree, people stocking up on petunias, privets and flowering plums and anything else they could get their hands on. Before I realized what was going on, I sold half my nursery stock. I locked my gates and when word got out, there was a run on the nursery not unlike the days after the Crash of '29. The police were called out to disperse the unruly mob, but I was blackmailed into paying them off with my last two flats of ivy.

That was then. Now, until my stock is replenished, I dare not sell any more plants. I don't know how long I can hold off, though. Crowds surround the nursery every day, trying to get a whiff of oxygen. Mothers hold their children up to the fence, begging me to let their little ones play in the nursery's sandbox. My stock is slowly disappearing to the police that are supposed to protect me. Our whole house is chock full of plants and trees, which is just barely enough oxygen to get us through the day.

The world is a nightmare. If only people had been more interested in horticulture and gardening years ago, maybe this awful tragedy could have been avoided. I often wonder now, as I watch the listless faces of the thinning crowds that come to watch my nursery every day, if it wasn't some premonition of the future, some precognitive memory buried deep in our subconscious of the longing, the desire, the almost frantic need to want to work in a nursery. Too late. Too late.

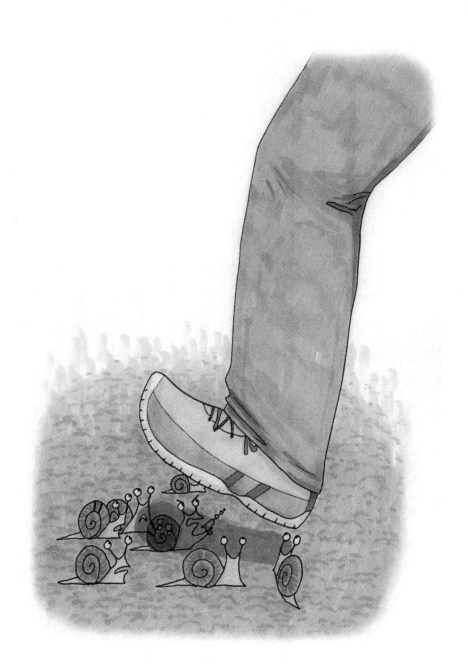

The Truth about Snails

Few people in the world know the true nature of our lowly California snails. They are militant flesh-eating aliens from another world. A strong statement, but one you will soon agree with. Most people know that snails are not native to California, but few know the real way they got here and their awful mission of conquest and consumption.

It all started early one morning at the home of the owner of Rising Sun Nursery, a humble yet cherished retail nursery in the foothills of Calaveras County. Don grew trees for the retail nursery at his home, which, because of their height and leaf canopy, was one of the reasons it was chosen as an entry point for invasion. Inside, Don was reading a book and eating a bowl of cereal—blissfully unaware.

"Commander Shlor, report!" demanded an impatient General Glosh. If he was going to subjugate the humans, he needed faster reports.

"General Glosh, sir!" The commander snapped a salute with his antenna, as he slithered up to the general.

The general responded by nonchalantly waving one antenna, and then extended the other and grabbed the report.

Shlor observed the general with concern. He usually kept that antenna withdrawn from view. The rumor was that maybe the general had a small bottle of booze tucked away, but Shlor knew that the general wanted to set himself apart from his men. Besides, it looked very dignified. Some of the young officers were beginning to emulate the general.

"Very good, Commander. It appears that all is ready to paralyze the human as he exits his dwelling. Once we have tasted his flesh and absorbed his DNA, we will be able to replicate his form at will and then soon I will rule this miserable little planet."

Commander Shlor eyed the general warily. Glosh was frothing around his shell and his antennae waved erratically in the air. Shlor was not entirely sure the general was completely sane. It didn't matter, though. After the human was absorbed, Shlor would be taking over. The general was going to have a little accident with some salt.

"General, sir. Request permission to go to the space ship and fire the paralyzing ray at the human."

"Why, certainly, Commander," said the general, who knew of Shlor's plans. "That is an excellent idea. You go right ahead. You deserve the honor." The general chuckled softly. Little did Shlor know that the general had a remote-control device to fire the ray. The ship's control panel would be useless.

Shlor smiled as he slithered away. This was better than he had hoped. With the paralyzing ray in his possession, he could take immediate control of the army. Little did General Glosh know that Shlor had deactivated the remote-control device.

As the time approached, the snails hunkered down in their shells awaiting the moment of attack. They glanced at pictures of their loved ones and then hastily stuffed them back under their shells. The ray was pointed at the door where, according to intelligence reports, the human would exit. The knob turned slowly, and the door inched open. This was it, then.

"I hope it won't be quite so hot today," Don said to Erin, his ten-year-old daughter, as he opened the door. "Will you be out soon? I want you to finish your chores before it gets too hot."

"Yeah, Dad." Erin stuffed another spoonful of cooked oatmeal in her mouth. "I need to finish weeding Section C."

"Okay." Don opened the door and stepped outside. The cool of the morning was delightful. Soft pink clouds dotted a pale blue sky. Another beautiful day.

"Attack!" screamed the general and he pressed the button on his remote control.

"Attack!" shouted the commander and he fired the ray. But nothing happened.

Don crunched on a snail, slipped on the slime, and fell heavily on top of the spaceship. Commander Shlor died instantly.

"Well, that's what Erin gets for leaving her toys out." Don picked up the crushed ship and tossed it into the garbage can. He brushed himself off and walked away.

A disorganized and terrified army oozed its way back to the general.

"What are we going to do, General? How will we survive?" asked a young recruit.

"Don't you remember your basic training?" snapped the general. "We must go underground until they send another ship to rescue us. Meanwhile, we must survive. We'll eat plants if we have to. But we must survive, multiply, and wait. Someday the humans will pay for this crime, and I will be there waiting to absorb them."

The Question

The sun was going down, and the nursery was empty of customers. Oliver had his books packed, a piece of grass stuck on his back for a light snack, and a nice shiny Pyracantha berry to give to the teacher. To get to school, he had to crawl the length of the shade house and meet behind the Camelia. His father was waiting for him at the front door of their house, which was just a drain hole in the bottom of a hollowed-out five-gallon Gardenia.

"Hurry up, Ollie," his father urged, tapping his antenna on the ground impatiently. "Just because you're a snail doesn't mean you can dawdle all day long."

Oliver slowly inched his way across the living room. It was his first day of school, and he was in no mood to end his summer vacation. He passed Grandpa, stuck to the inside of the pot and snoring softly with just a bit of foam bubbling on the edge of his shell.

"Why, when I was your age," his father went on, "we crawled a mile through thorny berry bushes to go to school. In the snow," his father added.

Oliver had never seen snow or berry bushes, so he could hardly compare his experience with his father's.

"What's that on your back? A piece of grass!" asked his father, prodding it with his antenna.

"Mom gave it to me for a snack."

"A piece of grass! Why, no self-respecting snail would be seen eating grass. Where's your mother? Myrtle? Why does Ollie have a piece of grass on his back?"

"But, Dad—"

"Not now, son. Myrtle!"

"Henry, for Pete's sake! What is all the yelling about? Ollie! Haven't you left for school yet?" asked Ollie's mother, poking her antenna out of the kitchen.

"That's just it," Henry raged. "Look. Grass on his back!"

"But Dad—"

"Certainly, we can afford better than grass for little Ollie."

"Henry, I didn't have time to crawl across the nursery to get some Hosta. Besides, Ollie *likes* grass. Now, if you don't mind, Ollie needs to get to school, and I have to clean up after Grandpa. He slimed the whole kitchen when he ate breakfast. I think he needs his dentures checked." And with that, Myrtle oozed back into the kitchen.

Henry turned to Oliver. "You like grass?"

"That's what I was trying to tell you, Dad."

Henry just rolled his antenna in disbelief and muttered, "You try to raise them right."

"Dad, I want to know," Oliver paused, not sure quite how to word it.

"Yes, son?"

"Is it true that snails can change their sex when there isn't enough of . . . um, the other kind around?"

Henry frowned. "Yes," he answered slowly, wondering where this was going.

"Dad, when I get to school, and I meet everyone," again Oliver paused.

"What is it, son? You just ask old dad."

"Well, you know how my new teacher, Miss Frum, who used to be Mr. Frum, changed into a lady because there weren't enough girl snails around?"

"Yes," said his father slowly again. He really didn't like where this was going. "There are *some* snails that can change their sex when called for. Certainly, nobody in *our* family has ever done that, and I hope you aren't getting any ideas that—"

"I don't want to do that, Dad. But, well, it's really confusing." Oliver sighed heavily. "I guess what I really want to know is this. How can I tell the girl snails from the boy snails? I mean, there doesn't seem to be any way to know unless they tell you. Is there something you can see or have to do to find out?"

Henry grinned and then chuckled a little as he looked down on little Ollie.

"Well, well. What an interesting question. Well, you see, you uh, you can tell by, uh . . . you see little girl snails have . . . and then little boy snails have, um."

He turned and put an antenna to his mouth, "Myrtle, get in here. Little Ollie wants to ask you a question."

The Horticulturalist

The police pulled up to the nursery and killed their siren. There was a long line of customers waiting to purchase their plants.

"It looks ugly, Ed."

Ed looked back at his partner, Joe, slender but well-built, short military haircut, all brawn and no brains—a typical rookie. Rookies were always jumping to conclusions. Ed had seen many a nurseryman crack over the years. The pressure, the hours, all the little old ladies asking the same questions over and over. He was glad that his father steered him away from the nursery business and into something less stressful like law enforcement.

"The word is sad, Joe."

Ed scanned the crowd. It didn't look that different from any other nursery situation he'd seen in the last twenty years. A blond lady, her nose red, with tears streaking down her cheeks, came running up to the squad car.

"Officer, my husband barricaded himself in the sales office. He's surrounded himself with plants. I . . . I don't know what he's going to do."

Ed looked grim. "Is he armed, ma'am?"

"Yes. He's got his Felco pruners."

"Felco's?" Ed repeated softly. Another hostage situation and here he was with a rookie as a backup.

"Um, Ed? What's a Felco?" Joe asked innocently.

Ed shot him a steely glare. "Felco pruners are the best in the business. You can cut a one-inch branch like it wasn't even there."

Joe looked scared. Ed knew that he couldn't count on Joe to handle this. No, this was his baby. Ed lifted his heavy body out of the car. He looked down at the worried lady standing next to him. "What's your husband's name?"

"It's Henry. Oh, officer! Will everything be all right?" she asked, and then broke down sobbing.

"Henry, the horticulturalist?" asked Joe. "I heard him on the radio. He was explaining how to prune—"

Ed shot Joe an annoyed glance. "Not now, Joe." He patted her gently on the shoulder. "We're in charge now."

Ed grabbed the megaphone and turned it on. It crackled to life.

"You people there. We have a hostage situation here. Please back slowly away from the building. We'll take over now."

A little old lady stomped her foot and refused to move. "He hasn't answered my question yet! There is some funny stuff on my rose and I want to know what he's going to do about it. After all, I bought it here!"

Ed heard a muffled sob inside the store. He knew he didn't have much time.

"Back off! All you people. Come on. Move it," Ed snapped. "Joe, keep them back."

"Well! I never," huffed the little old lady, but she and several others stepped back while craning their necks to see.

Ed called out. "I'm coming in now, Henry. Don't do anything that we'll both regret. I'm coming in now, nice and slowly."

He eased the shop door open and glanced quickly around the room. Henry, his hair askew, was huddled in the corner, a Dracaena clasped tightly in his left hand. A Felco pruner in Henry's right hand was opened and surrounding the neck of the plant. Ed saw the Felco's shaking slightly and Henry's dazed, wild-animal look. Ed could tell right away, he'd seen dozens of killers and murderers, and Henry wasn't one. Oh, he might be able to throw out old or diseased plants now and then while they were still alive, but to outright kill a perfectly healthy plant? Nah, it wasn't in him. It looked like Henry hadn't shaved in a few days. Poor guy.

"Don't come any closer," Henry warned.

"Henry, you don't really want to hurt that plant. Come on. Put the Felco's down and let's talk about it."

"No! I'm tired of talking about plants. You don't know what it's like. Every party you go to, people ask you questions about plants. At the bank they do and the grocery store. Even at the theater in the dark, someone recognized me and whispered a plant question. I . . . I just can't take it anymore."

"We can talk about football if you like or maybe fishing or boating or—"

"Fi . . . fishing?" Henry stammered, his eyes blinking rapidly.

"Yes, fishing. Where do you like to fish? What do you like to fish for?"

Henry's eyes narrowed. "You're trying to trick me. You don't really care about fishing."

"Are you kidding?" Ed chuckled. "I love to fish. I went just last Saturday with my friend, Bill. Maybe you could join us sometime. I have this boat and it fits three easy." Ed continued talking about bait, hooks and reels until he noticed that Henry's right hand was slowly dropping with the clippers resting on his lap. The plant was out of danger. Now, if he could just get those Felco's away from Henry before anything happened.

"Should I fertilize my petunias now, or wait until after my grandson's birthday party?" asked an elderly woman, popping her head through the doorway.

"Get out!" ordered Ed. "Joe, I told you to keep them away. Joe?" But Joe didn't answer. *What was going on out there?* Ed turned back to Henry and sighed in frustration. Henry's eyes were glazed over again, and the clippers were back on the Dracaena. Ed's eyes widened. This time there was some sap oozing out of the stem. Perhaps it was just Henry's shaking hand, perhaps he didn't mean to hurt the plant.

"Leave me, or one by one all the plants in here will suffer the same fate," Henry said in a faraway voice, and then he snipped the Dracaena in two. Half of the plant fell to the floor.

Quick as lightning, before Ed could react, Henry grabbed another plant, this time a Pothos. Ed backed up slowly, his open palms up in the air and went out the front door. Outside was chaos. Joe was being overwhelmed by irate customers. It was spring after all.

"I just wanted a bag of peat moss," yelled a heavy-set man, who was trying to push his way past Joe.

Ed ran to the squad care and requested immediate backup as well as a SWAT team.

"And send an ambulance and a horticulturalist now!" He had heard what happened to other officers who failed to stop a riot at their local nursery.

Soon police cars came screaming into the nursery parking lot. The SWAT team began putting on their bulletproof vests. Quickly the subdued crowd was pushed back.

"What's the status, Ed?" asked the captain, frowning and looking around nervously. He and Ed went way back and there was mutual trust and respect between them.

"He's lost it, Bob. I'd send the SWAT team in right away. He's already killed one plant. Who knows how many more may suffer the same fate?"

The captain winced. Ed knew his dilemma. Already two nursery owners had cracked this year and it was only early June. The police commissioner's wife was an avid gardener and complained that the captain was too heavy-handed. On the other hand, could he afford to wait while plants died as they were standing there?

"Okay, Ed, we'll send them in. I just want you to try and talk him down one more time before we send the team in."

"Excuse me," said a small voice. The men turned around and looked down at a young girl about college age. Her long red hair was tied back, and her bright blue eyes looked up at them anxiously. "I was told that you needed a horticulturalist."

The men looked at her doubtfully.

98

"I have a B.S. degree from Cal Poly in Environmental Horticulture. I just graduated a couple weeks ago."

"I thought it was called Ornamental Horticulture," Ed said flatly, clearly not convinced.

The girl smiled. "That was a *long* time ago," she said. "They changed the name."

"Okay," said the captain, in no position to argue. "We have a Dracaena down and a Pothos in danger. Do you have any recommendations?"

"Sure," answered the girl matter-of-factly. "If he cuts any of them, we can just propagate them. Just use some rooting hormone. None of the plants have to die, and the ones he cuts will just re-sprout. Actually, we did it all the time in our propagation class."

Ed slapped his forehead. Why hadn't he thought of that? The captain eyed him with disgust. He looked at the SWAT team and jabbed a thumb in the direction of the nursery. The men ran into the shop. There was a short burst of yelling, then a crash. Soon they led Henry out, his head bowed and turned away from the crowd.

"I never did think he was that great of a nurseryman," remarked one woman.

"I think he gave me the wrong answer a few years ago," stated another lady.

"He sold me a plant that he said was supposed to be deer resistant, and it wasn't," complained an elderly man.

"What did he say about that?" asked a lady standing next to him.

"He said deer can't read," scoffed the elderly man.

Another woman listening just shook her head in disgust.

"He sold me a Chinese evergreen elm and it lost most of its leaves during that real cold snap last year," said a mother, holding onto her two young children.

"Did it come out of it?" asked a lady.

"Yes," she answered. "But that's not the point."

They watched angrily as Henry was put in the back of a squad car, his hands covering his face. Quickly the police roared off, leaving just Ed and Joe at the nursery. The crowd began to disperse. Ed handed the girl a bag of cuttings—the ones cut off in the scuffle with Henry.

"Do you want a lift back home?" Ed asked

"No. Thank you," she said curtly. "I would like to look around the nursery, if you don't mind."

Ed heaved himself into the squad car, and he and Joe sped away. Henry's distraught wife said she would close the nursery for the day. Their job was done.

The crowd watched her silently for a moment. Heads turned as she walked by. Then someone shouted out, "What's the difference between a Japanese and a Silver Maple?"

And with that, they were on her.

The Fastest in the West

Don could hear the piano player banging the keys and the rumble of men gambling and laughing as he crossed the dusty street and sauntered toward the saloon.

He pushed on the swinging doors and headed for the bar. Tex Brisco glanced up from his cards and noticed the powerful six-foot-one, 200-pound frame with the Felco pruners tied low on his hip. His mouth went dry. He shot a quick glance at his buddy, Tommy Fox, but Tommy was already staring.

"He's the fastest—" Tommy started.

"I know, I know," Tex snapped irritably.

"But isn't he the owner of the Rising Sun?" Tommy added.

"Yes. And he always prunes to an outside bud. I'd like to see that for myself," Tex said sourly. "One day he's going to cut off more than he can chew."

Halfway to the bar the piano stopped playing and suddenly the only sound was Don's boots echoing on the wooden floor. Don pushed up to the bar and said, "Rye." The bartender nervously filled a shot glass while Don carefully surveyed the room reflected in the large mirror on the wall behind the bar. He downed the whiskey in one gulp and slammed it on the bar. "Another."

The pretty barmaid, Leeanne, was watching too.

"Can I help you with anything else, Mr. Urbanus?"

Don turned around and for a moment he forgot what he came to do. There stood the prettiest little filly a man ever set eyes on. Her little turned up nose and high cheekbones were well formed and her hair, piled up on her head, showed her graceful neck. She smiled, and Don sank into those soft brown eyes. He couldn't help noticing, glancing at her curvy figure, that she was all a man would ever need and then some. But that wasn't why he was here.

Don tipped his hat. "Please call me Don, ma'am. I'm here to hire a couple good men."

Ed Baxter, the grizzly owner of Nurseryland West, stood up and faced Don. He was short but built like a mule. There was poison is his eyes. "I know you. You think you're so high and mighty winning Best Nursery of Calaveras County and then the next year, Best Nursery in the Mother Lode. Well, I'm here to tell you that I'm taking over this range. I'm running you out of this county and when it happens, you'll be the first to know."

Don grinned. "That a fact? I got over fifteen-hundred customers signed up on my email newsletter with links to my website. I write gardening articles for the *Lodestar*. I just gave a class on pruning fruit trees. Nobody is running me out of this county." He turned back to his drink.

Ed tugged on Don's arm. "I'm talking to you."

Don turned but he wasn't smiling anymore. His hand instinctively went down near his clippers. His eyes went cold.

Baxter licked his lips and blinked. He didn't want a direct confrontation. There were other ways to handle this. More devious ways. He could wait his turn. Baxter took a step back. "I'm just saying. You've been warned."

Don stood tall and faced Baxter. "You can take your big box store and put it where the sun don't shine, Baxter. I'm staying."

Baxter's face turned crimson, but he stayed silent.

Dave and Randy Willet were sitting at the bar. They worked for Baxter, but they didn't like him. They didn't like him at all. There was something about the tall man with the Felco pruners that they liked.

Randy spoke first, "I'm Randy, and this here is my brother Dave. We're looking for work. We'd be proud to work for the Rising Sun."

Ed turned his head slowly, glaring at Randy. "You'll never work for another Nurseryland in California if you do."

Dave grinned and stood up. He pushed his hat back on his head. "Why, Mr. Baxter, whatever gave you the idea that we wanted to work at another Nurseryland? We're giving our two weeks notice."

"Save your breath. You're both fired. Now get out of my saloon." He turned and sat back down at his table. Some of his hired help got up and stared hard at Dave and Randy.

Don faced them down. "Now, that's no way to treat your employees, Mr. Baxter. I was just buying them a drink. When we're done, we'll leave this joint and not before."

Leanne looked from Don to the other men confronting him.

"That's okay, Mr. Urbanus," Randy said softly. "We don't want to cause any trouble. We just want to work for you."

"Sit down, boys," Baxter growled. "Let 'em have their drink. It's a free country." ·

"Much obliged, Mr. Baxter." Don nodded at the bartender who poured two whiskeys and shoved them toward the men. Then he turned to face Dave and Randy. "Just call me Don. What are you guys packing?"

Dave eagerly produced his pruners. "They're not new, but they're sharp."

Don looked them over. *Red Roosters. A new brand.* They felt good in his hand. He opened them and reached over and sliced a menu at the bar. It cut it like scissors.

Randy added, "They're Komodos and very ergonomic."

"Sharp," Don said, impressed. He handed them back to Dave.

"I know they aren't the most expensive pruners, but a great buy for the money," Dave replied.

"I got the same clippers as Dave," Randy added.

"People are always looking for great value, Dave. You can start first thing Monday morning. You too, Randy."

Dave and Randy looked at each other and flashed a smile. "Sure thing, Don. We'll see you then. Come on, Randy. Let's get out of here."

Dave and Randy downed their whiskey, grinned, and headed out while Ed Baxter glared at them. He would take care of those two as well. He had his ways.

Don turned to walk out, too, when his eyes met Leeanne's. He smiled and his whole face lit up. Leeanne caught her breath and raised her hand to rest on her heart. He touched his hat. "Ma'am. I'm sure we'll meet again."

"I'm sure we will, Don." Her eyes lingered on him as he strode across the bar and left. She turned and saw Ed Baxter watching her, his face red with fury like a pressure cooker about to explode.

"He doesn't own me," she muttered angrily, as she vigorously wiped a table. She paused and looked thoughtfully at the door Don had just exited, smiled, and went back to wiping the table.

Any Complaints?

The sun was rising rapidly in a cloudless sky. She knew that the burning sun would soon finish her off. Yet she lay there, sprawled out on the gravel road, unable to move. All night long she struggled to get away. She knew now she wasn't going to make it.

Why did she listen to the others? Many left in the large white truck and never came back. Did that mean they were sent to their deaths? Who knew where they went and what happened to them. All this talk of being mistreated was pure bunk. She knew that now. They were given food and water every day. Did they get that on the outside?

She should have been content, and yet, she felt so restricted, so confined. Her break for freedom seemed so clear back then. How wrong she had been. She tried to lift herself up and fell back down, exhausted.

After she was dead, she knew what would happen. She saw them coming for the dead and sick. They were put on carts and dumped carelessly in piles with the other rotting corpses. Please, let her die here and now. Please, God, not on that pile.

She was dry and thirsty. What little strength she had had wilted away. The warm sun was taking its toll. Delirious, her thoughts wandered back to when she was little and happy—it seemed so long ago.

She felt, rather than heard, the footsteps coming closer. Large boots crushed the gravel and then stopped next to her. This was it then. She didn't care anymore. She just didn't care.

A man bent over and roughly picked her up.

"Who the hell left this Agapanthus out in the sun and where is its damned pot?" muttered the man.

He went to the soil pile and grabbed a one-gallon pot, but he couldn't stuff the Agapanthus back in.

"That will never fit."

He grabbed a couple more pots and then set the plant on the workbench and tore at the roots, dividing the plant into three. Quickly, he put the pieces into the new pots and added fresh soil and fertilizer. He carried the plants back to the shade house and put them down with the others and watered them. Then he walked away, whistling.

The plants sat there soaking up the water.

"Any complaints?" asked one.

"Not me. Not me," answered the other two.

Plant Court Justice

Plant Court was in session with the Honorable Marsha Mayfield presiding. Lawyers feared her. She was a no-nonsense judge who had worked at a nursery to pay her way through college. She reluctantly quit her job and got a loan to pay for law school. There was no easy way to buffalo Marsha when it came to plants. If you got Marsha for your judge, the best thing to do was plead guilty and try to bargain with her.

But not every lawyer was that smart.

Marsha gazed dourly at a scared Sally Preston, a thirtyish perky-looking, so-called public relations officer for a local garden club. Sally had left for a vacation on a Caribbean cruise for ten days. In her excitement at being asked on the cruise by the club president, Sally completely forgot to set the automatic timer on her new landscape.

Sitting in the audience was a rather ashen-looking Ralph Clark, the club president. Next to Ralph was planted prim Abby Murphy, the club treasurer, who had not been asked on the cruise. Marsha noticed her pursed mouth and occasional hostile glances at Ralph.

When Sally returned from the cruise, her plants were fried. Sally belonged to a garden club. She should have known better. This little episode of plant abuse had landed her in court— Marsha's court. How Marsha loved her job.

Right now, Sally's lawyer was digging her grave big enough to plant a boxed tree in. An experienced plant lawyer might make a case that Sally had mulched her plants or that the automatic clock was new or might have malfunctioned.

"So, it's true, Miss Preston, that you *meant* to water your plants and that you didn't *want* your plants to die?" Sally's lawyer asked hopefully. Marsha thought she heard the lawyer for the prosecution snicker. She'd have to talk to him later.

Sally glanced nervously at Marsha and around the room.

"Please answer the question, Miss Preston," Marsha monotoned.

Sally gulped. "Yes, of course I *meant* to water the plants. That's why I got the automatic timer. I just . . . I just forgot in the rush to get ready for my cruise."

"The defense rests your Honor," Sally's lawyer offered.

Marsha took a deep breath. "Normally, I might take a recess to review the case. But this is just a blatant disregard for your plants and clear case of vegetative abuse. Obviously, your focus was *not* on your plants." She glanced quickly at Ralph Clark, who withered under her glare. "I fine you $1000 and order you to attend fifty hours of classes at your local nursery, where, I hope, you might find a little more appreciation for plants. While you were floating on an ocean of water, Miss Preston, your plants were dying of thirst. You may step down, Miss Preston."

Sally looked shaken, but she stood and faced the judge. "Yes, Your Honor. I'm sorry. I'll try to do better."

"Tell that to the plants that died." Marsha had little sympathy for killers of greenery. She slammed her gavel down. "Next case."

Sally's lawyer consoled her and guided her out of the court. A few people shook their heads as she was leaving. A concerned and frowning Ralph stood up to leave. Next to him, Abby Murphy smiled radiantly.

The bailiff stood up. "The next case is Anderson vs. Rising Sun Nursery."

The judge smiled. Usually the owner of the nursery was testifying *for* the prosecution. This was going to be interesting.

Ed Thomas, a lawyer hired by Marian Anderson, stood up. "We call Don Urbanus, the owner of Rising Sun Nursery to the stand, Your Honor."

A tall and tanned man stood up and walked with a slight limp to the stand.

"My client states that you sold her a defective maple tree that died in less than a week, Mr. Urbanus. She brought it back to your store and you were very rude, accusing her of plant neglect. And you refused to stand behind your product and kicked her out of your nursery. Why would you do that, sir?"

"Objection, Your Honor." A snappy-looking woman stood up. It was Don's lawyer, Lisa Howard, horticulturalist on retainer for the state. "That is a leading question."

"Sustained. Restate your question, counselor."

Thomas coughed and took a breath. "Mr. Urbanus, is it true that you sold my client a defective tree that died a week later?"

"No. It is not true. The tree she brought back wasn't dead, although I did decline to replace it."

"And why was that, Mr. Urbanus? Isn't it your policy to replace defective merchandise?"

"The tree in question was not defective, it was bone dry. Marian hadn't watered the tree in almost a week in the middle of June."

"It rained one day during the week," Marian screamed out. "And then that idiot started watering it when I told him I wanted to take it home. How am I supposed to take a tree home if it's leaking water all over the place!"

Marsha banged the gavel repeatedly, but not before Marian had her say.

"Mrs. Anderson. One more outburst like that and you will be in contempt of court!"

Marian clamped her mouth shut and sat down in a huff.

The judge looked over at Don. "Continue, Mr. Urbanus."

"Our policy doesn't include a guarantee if the plants are not watered. Marian, Mrs. Anderson, said she would never shop at our store again and marched out. *That's* when I watered the maple tree."

"You're saying my client left without the tree? That's seems highly irregular."

"Yes, she left, but then decided that she would take the tree after all. By then I had watered it. That's when she yelled at me to 'Stop watering it!'" A ripple of laughter fluttered through the courtroom.

Mrs. Anderson stood up, but then thought better of it and sat back down.

"You are claiming that the tree wasn't dead, Mr. Urbanus? How can you be so sure?"

"Just from almost 40 years in the nursery business. It looked like it still had some life to it. The branches were still supple and plump, although the leaves were in bad shape. I thought it would come back. So, I watered it."

"But the tree died anyway, Mr. Urbanus. And it died because you—"

"Oh, it didn't die."

"What?"

"It's still alive. Marian and her husband planted it. It's coming out nicely. I drive by it every day on my way to work." Don looked over at Marian, smiled, and then waved.

Marian snarled, "It was as good as dead."

"Counselors, please approach the bench." Marsha was furious. Ed and Lisa walked up to the bench. The judge directed her ire at Ed. "Ed, didn't you check to see if her damn tree was dead or not?"

"I'm sorry, Your Honor. I just took her word for it. I'm not an expert on trees."

Marsha fumed. "Yes, but we *have* an expert on trees and he's sitting in the witness stand."

Lisa smiled. "I make a motion to dismiss, Your Honor."

"Case dismissed." Marsha banged the gavel down. "You're excused, Mr. Urbanus. Sorry that we wasted your time."

Don stood up and walked off the stand. His lawyer patted him on the back and said a few encouraging words. A woman popped up to ask a plant question before he could leave. The judge watched with respect and admiration as he answered the question and then walked out of the court. Then she went grim and ripped into Marian, giving her a lesson on watering plants and wasting the court's time.

It was all so unnecessary, she thought. If they only listened to their local nursery professional, so many plant fines could be avoided. Plant abuse would be a thing of the past. But then she might be out of a job.

No, there would always be plant abusers and vegetation neglecters. More plants would die from negligence and ignorance. She would be the last wall of defense for the defenseless—the watering can of the courts bringing relief to a thirsty green world. All she could do was even the balance sheet.

And, oh, how she loved to do that.

The Last Nursery

Erin slowly straightened her back and peeled the gloves off her bony hands. She flexed her digits slowly. At ninety-five-years old, she realized that weeding was no easy task, but she was determined to get Rising Sun Nursery ready for its centennial anniversary in April of 2088. It had been a hundred years since her beloved father had started the nursery. She always saw him as being younger in her mind, in his late forties or early fifties. But she had been a girl then. Everything seemed more alive in the past.

Somehow, she kept the nursery going after her father's passing. Her own son had run it for more than twenty years, but he was retired now. Much had changed over the years. Much had stayed the same.

She glanced disdainfully at the youthful protesters holding digital placards and gesturing violently in sign language. Every generation had to have their own form of rebellion. The current trend was not to talk to any authority figure.

Erin had seen it all—shaved hair, long hair, no hair, purple hair, burnt hair, baggy clothes, tight clothes, no clothes, you name it. This talking in sign language about keeping her plants prisoners in pots and wanting to set them free really ticked her off. She was getting angry enough to give them a little sign language of her own.

All this attention was focused on her because she owned the last retail nursery in California. These high-tech cyberpunks ate their synthesized, hydrolyzed, homogenized and double-wrapped yeast bars and lived in their virtual holographic whatevers, and they dared to tell her that keeping plants in pots was cruel and not natural?

They could *have* their computerized vinyl landscapes that could be programmed to bloom on command. The colors of the leaves and flowers could be changed quickly to fit a person's mood or whim. They even gave out degrees in landscape design in something that didn't use real plants anymore. She shuddered. Everything was instant gratification these days. No more waiting patiently for your petunias to bloom and then have a late frost or hungry snails ruin them. It was disgusting.

She tightened the strap under her chin to keep her hat secure, then put her gloves back on. Grabbing a cart, she loaded a dozen one-gallon plants she had propagated especially for an occasion such as this—plants that really needed to be "set free."

She wheeled up to the gate, opened it, and pushed the cart into the gesturing mob. They descended upon the plants while she backed up and slowly closed the gate. They knocked the pots off the imprisoned plants and shouted for joy in sign language, marching away triumphantly stroking and caressing each leaf of the freed inmates.

Erin scrunched up her old face into a contented smile as she watched them leave. She rolled the cart into the nursery and absentmindedly reached into her sweater pocket and tossed some labels into the garbage can.

Her great-granddaughter, Astra, her live-in help, watched the whole scene with great interest.

"Grannie, you *never* give anything away free—especially plants and never to those nuts."

"Astra, I think I'll go lie down for a little bit. I'm tired."

"Sure, Grannie, I'll finish up the weeding. You just rest for a while."

After Erin went around a corner, Astra quickly looked in the garbage can for a label. She plucked one out. Something was written in pencil. It didn't mean anything to her. She waved her phone over the label.

"Identify."

A soft feminine voice answered, "*Rhus diversiloba,* an archaic form of *Toxicodendron diversilobum.*"

Astra sighed. "Yes, but what is it exactly?"

"Oh, sorry, Astra. It is commonly known as Western Poison Oak. Is there anything else you need?"

Astra giggled and looked up to see her great-grandmother looking down at her from an upstairs window, smiling, and Astra grinned back.

Quips and Queries from the Nursery Trenches

Is a retail nursery as wonderful as you think it is? Yes and no. It's a lot harder than you think and it is physical work—unloading trucks, loading soil into a customer's vehicle, lifting 15-gallon trees. Often your hands, arms, or legs are nicked, cut, or bruised. You get slivers all the time. I have scars all over my hands and arms. Sometimes your back aches. And yet, it's a lot of fun, too, especially if you have an eye for beauty. It's the best part-time job a person could ever want—if only I worked part-time.

Plants don't normally talk. Even when they are dying from thirst, most people don't hear them. I do. But then I can pick out a screaming plant with three hands tied behind my back—just ask the employees. "This is dry, you know?" "Did you water these today?" "Hey, water these, they're dry!" If you can't recognize when a plant needs water, don't work in a nursery.

If you don't like the public, you shouldn't be in retail. People are a kick. Challenging sometimes, but always interesting. I'm usually surprised about some of the things they ask about, or some of the darnedest things they say. I have collected what they've commented about and asked my employees to collect the conversations. Most of these snippets were written on little pieces of paper and stuffed into a file. Not everything that happened was funny, but who wants to hear bad stuff that occurred? I want to laugh—or at least chuckle about some of them. I hope you get a few chuckles out of this, too.

And yes, it's true. Not only can I flip my clippers, I can do a double flip, with open clippers, catch them by the handle, and flip them into my holster. I'm fast on the draw, too.

I Love Working in a Nursery

Susan loved working at the nursery. She didn't normally help pot up plants, but we had a lot of bareroot roses to pot up. She considered it a treat.

"Hey, Susan. Label the roses for me. It will be good training for you if you ever start dating again."

Susan is divorced but attractive with a nice figure. She looks at me like I've lost my mind. Later I hear her as she's labeling. "Ouch. Let go of me! Stop that!"

Deloni was patiently taking a customer around to the roses. The lady would stop and smell each flower. She just couldn't decide. There were just so many to choose from.

"Could you show me the roses once more?"

"Again? Um, sure. Okay." So around they went again with the lady stopping and smelling each rose. Deloni was hoping to get a sale since she was spending so much time with her.

"Would you like to get one of the roses?" Deloni asked hopefully.

"No, thank you. I just can't decide," she said. She started to walk away and then stopped. "You know, you have a great job. I've always wanted to work in a nursery. I could smell the flowers *all* day!"

I hired Louis when I first started my wholesale nursery. He was sixty-nine. I was a bit concerned about his age. I explained that he would be potting up plants, pruning, staking, and helping me load trucks.

"Do you think you can handle that kind of work?"

"Who me? You bet. I worked for Mother's Cookies. I'd unload the whole semi by myself. I can keep up. I can work in the mornings. I need my afternoon nap."

Louis was so good, I gave him a raise after the first day he worked for me. He practically ran while he worked. Turns out that Louis was a short Swiss dynamo who went dancing almost every weekend. I was lucky to keep up with Louis.

After a couple years working for me, we potted up some 5-gallon plants. These plants needed less water, so I told Louis to use the plastic low flow brown spitters in the pots instead of the medium flow green or high flow black spitters. The spitters spray out water when the valve comes on automatically.

The next day I noticed brown, green, and black spitters all mixed up in the pots.

"Hey, Louis. I told you to put brown spitters in the pots. They're all mixed up."

"Yeah? Sorry about that. I couldn't tell them apart."

"What do you mean? I said I wanted brown spitters."

"Oh, brown? Well, I'm color blind. They all looked the same to me."

"But you've worked for me for a couple years. You never said anything about being color blind. How do you tell stuff apart when you're pruning?"

"I kind of figure it out."

"Kind of? Holy cow! I wish I knew that when I hired you."

"Hey, I'm already old. I didn't want to be discriminated against because I'm color blind, too."

Louis worked for me until he was eighty-seven. He finally decided maybe he'd had enough. A couple years later I called him up and left a message for him to call me. Reluctantly, he called me back.

"Yeah, Don? What do you need?"

"I wanted to invite you and your girlfriend over for dinner."

"Oh, that's a relief. I thought you wanted me to come back to work."

(How many eighty-nine-year-olds do you know who are worried about going back to work if their old boss calls them?)

Pete was between jobs doing sheetrock and he was visiting his mother, so I hired him. He became my rose expert, pruning and dead-heading them. Because he lived down the street from the nursery, he was able to walk to work. Still, Pete would often be a few minutes late. One day he was an hour late.

Frustrated, I confronted him. "What's this? An *hour* late?"

"Give me a break. I haven't been laid in a year and a half." (I've heard *lots* of excuses over the years for being late. Now *that's* an excuse.)

Pete came back to California from Oklahoma because his mother had terminal cancer.

"You know, I think this was the best job I ever had. I sure do miss those roses."

"You did a great job on those roses. They never looked so good."

"I have a favor to ask of you."

"Sure, Pete. What do you need?"

"Can I borrow your circular saw, and do you have any spare wood or plywood?"

"Sure. What are you going to make?"

"A casket. I figure she's not going to last. I'll just take her back home to Oklahoma and throw some dry ice on her."

"Is that legal?"

"Who cares? It's my mother. I can do what I want with her."

Pete builds his casket at the nursery. A plywood box with a lid.

Fortunately, his mother went into remission, and he was able to drive her home in the front seat of his pickup instead of the back.

Judy has worked for me from the very beginning when I first opened the retail nursery. She used to run a nursery in the next county when the owner died. The new owner was cutting her hours back, so I snatched her up.

A year later, I hired John. Trying to look respectable, he shaved off his mountain-man beard, but promptly started growing it back once I hired him. John liked to talk and could go on and on.

"Keep him away from me, he's driving me crazy," Judy said on a number of occasions.

A couple of months later, one of the other employees mentioned that Judy and John were dating.

"But that's impossible. She can't stand him," I said.

"Oh, Don," Dinea smirked. "Don't you pay attention at all?"

"The boss is always the last to know," Shelly agreed.

"They've been dating for weeks," Dinea informed me.

"But she said she couldn't stand him," I protested. They just shook their heads sadly at me that I could be so unobservant.

Who would have thought that I would become a matchmaker? Judy and John have been together for twenty years.

After almost four years working at the nursery, John started his own maintenance company.

Job Applicants

Applicant for nursery job calls on the phone: "Where are you located, anyway?"

Second applicant for nursery job calls on the phone: "What exactly do you guys do?"

Job interview: "Hello. Are you here for the job application?" I look at my watch. He's an hour late for his appointment.

"Yeah."

"And your name is?"

"Greg. I'm living with my aunt and uncle right now and my aunt said I had to get a job. My uncle drove me over here. It's the only car we have in the house, or I would have been here sooner."

"Okay. Well, here is the application. You can sit right here and fill it out."

After a few minutes, Greg stood up. "I'm finished. Say, how much do you pay here?"

"It depends on experience. If you don't have any, we usually start at minimum wage." I look at the application. There are no previous jobs or personal references filled out. I bring it to his attention.

"Oh, I don't remember all that stuff."

"Well, how am I supposed to compare you with other applicants if you don't fill this out?"

"I could take it home and fill it out."

"That would be fine."

An hour later, Greg shows back up.

"Hi. I'm back. Boy, I don't feel very well though. My stomach is upset. I guess I drank too much last night. Maybe it was mixing champagne, beer and vodka."

"Yeah. That will do it. I see you've filled out the rest of the application. I won't be deciding until the end of next week. Thanks for coming by."

Another job interview: A guy in his early forties, hands me his application. He is wearing a tank top and has numerous tattoos on his shoulders. His cap is on backwards and he is missing a couple teeth.

"I want you to know that it wasn't my fault."

"It wasn't your fault about what?" I ask.

"Getting fired from my last job."

"Oh, I see. Why did you get fired?" I ask, scanning the application.

"I couldn't get to work."

"You couldn't get to work?"

"Yeah. Because I was in jail. I couldn't get to work, so they fired me."

"Why were you in jail?"

"Because of the DUI. The cops arrested me and threw me in jail."

"You got a DUI?"

"Yeah, but that was weeks ago. Nothing has happened since then."

"Okay. Well, thanks for dropping off the application."

"I've always wanted to work in a nursery. If you ever have an opening, let me know!" said about a hundred middle-aged women. (And guess who gets hired the most.)

Do You Mind if I …?

Guy comes in and wants to cut all the roses off our five-gallon plants we are selling. His daughter is getting married this weekend.

"Having roses on the plants is what sells them," I explain. "If you cut them all off, people won't buy them."

"Won't they grow back?"

Guy had a drug-hunting dog.

"Would it be okay if I hid drugs in the nursery for the dog to find? It would be good practice for him." (No. I don't like that idea.)

A tall guy in his forties named Dave wandered in off the street.

"Could I borrow $20 to buy some boots, so I can get this job. If I don't have the boots, I don't get the job."

I figured that I would never see the money again, but I made him write out a little promissory note. Almost exactly three months later, he came in and paid one of the employees. He left an apology note. "Sorry for taking so long to pay you back. Thanks, Dave."

An older customer comes in and starts looking in the bedding plants. After a while, he steps over to the bushes nearby, zips his fly down, and starts peeing. The lady employees make a big fuss and want me to confront him.

"You know, we have a bathroom right there in the breezeway."

"Yeah, I know, but I was never going to make that. You don't mind, do you?"

While Erin was minding the pond area, a customer's little boy peed in our fish pond. His mother didn't scold him. Instead she just asked him why he did that. He answered, "I don't know." Erin wasn't very happy about the liquid addition to her pond. (But I was a little boy once, and watching the water spill into the pond, I kind of know why he did it.)

Can You Get This?

A lady wanted some Johnny Jump-up violas. I told her they were called Helen Mount now and that they were the same thing. "I will wait until you get them in," she said.

A lady wanted bone marrow for her bulbs.
"We only carry bone meal."
"Okay, but I really wanted bone marrow."

A man wanted to know if we could get Palomino manure. "Things grow really well with it."

"Do you have any cherry trees?"
"Sure. Lots of them. What variety were you looking for?"
"I need something that is about two feet tall."
"Two feet tall? We don't have anything *that* short. Why does it have to be two feet tall?"
"I'm driving to Texas and I need to put it in my open pickup. I figured if it was only two feet tall, it would be fine back there."

"Can I get a bag of cow manure please? And how much is it?"
"Steer manure is $1.99 for a cubic foot."
"You don't have cow manure?"
"Steer manure is the same as cow manure."
"Oh, no. I want cow manure. If you don't have cow manure, then I'll go somewhere else."

A man inquired, "Why don't you carry Bougainvilleas?"
"Because they don't grow here."
"What do you mean? I just planted one that I bought at Lowe's and it's doing fine."
"Yes, *now*. But they don't make it through the winter."

A guy came in and asked for a fuzz-less peach.

"We have nectarines in stock."

"No," he said. "I want a peach."

Hispanic lady looking for 'original' for cooking. None of the employees know what 'original' is or what she is talking about. She uses it in all her cooking, and she's bought from us before. I walk over to the herbs and grab an oregano.

"This what you're looking for?"

"Oh, yes. Thank you!"

Guy wants to buy a Zen garden like in a kit or something for Christmas. It was on his girlfriend's list. He wanted to know what it was.

"It's something you make out of rocks and sand, making waves in the sand, and pretending the rocks are like islands," I tell him.

He laughs and says, "That's weird."

"I need a weeping flowering tree, but I only want it to get four feet tall. Got anything like that?"

"It wouldn't be a tree if it only got four feet tall. We have some bushes and even roses trained like a tree. We call them Patio trees."

"But they're not trees?"

"Not technically. They are just trained like a tree."

"No. I want a tree."

"Do you have any Copacabana?"

I handed her a plant with white flowers. "You mean a Bacopa?"

"Oh yes. That's it."

A guy wanted a bag of triple fifteen fertilizer. I told him we sell a triple sixteen. His wife said, "We struck out again. Let's get out of here."

A lady calls the store. She wants a vine but not sure what vine. Judy reads off a list of all the vines we carry.

"Don't you just have a vine vine?" she asks.

Asian guy comes into the store. He has a very thick accent.

"I like to see Raywoods, please."

I take him up to see the Raywood ash trees. He shakes his head. It's not what he wants. He is trying to explain what Raywoods are. We wander around the nursery looking for what he wants.

"Ah, there!" he points. He smiles and points to some trees— redwoods.

"Can I help you?" Anna said to a concerned lady holding a Tupperware container.

"I have a rather unusual request, but I thought this was the place to come."

"What do you need?"

"I would like to buy a dozen snails."

"Snails? You mean live snails?"

"Yes. I am a teacher and I need them for a class project."

"We don't *sell* snails. We kill them. What are you going to do with snails?" Anna laughed.

"We number their shells and race them," she replied.

"If you can find any snails, you can have them." (And unfortunately, she did.)

"Can I help you?"

"Yes. Do you carry light bulbs that give filtered light?" a lady asked.

"Filtered light?"

"Yes. I was reading in a book that lots of plants like filtered light."

A lady came into our store saying that a guy at Lowe's told her we had what she wanted. She wanted K-2 sprinklers. I told her we didn't carry those, but Lowe's should have them.

"Why are you guys always stonewalling me?"

"I need a restricted chemical shipped to Reno. Can you do that?"

"No. If it's restricted, we can't get it let, alone ship it."

"No? How about if you shipped it directly from the manufacturer?"

People Unclear on the Concept

The nursery is in full spring mode. Trucks are coming in every week. The nursery is full and bursting with color. A customer writes me a note. "When are you going to get fresh stock in?" (Why does this annoy me so much?)

Had a landscaper come in to buy seed for a lawn. Then he put a good dose of pre-emergent on the newly planted lawn to make sure he didn't get any weeds.

"Your lawn seed is defective. Hardly anything came up."

This guy's lemon tree has one vigorous branch full of big thorns in the middle of his bush.

"You need to cut that thorny branch out. It's from the rootstock. It will take over the whole tree."

"But it's so healthy! I can't believe I need to cut it out."

"If you don't, the rest of the lemon will suffer."

"I'm going to wait and see what kind of fruit I'll get on it first."

A lady got some cut roses for her mother's funeral. She came in to buy some rooting hormone to see if she could root them. About a month or so later she came back, very excited. She clasped her hands together and looked skyward. "They rooted! It was a miracle!"

Some people get confused when it comes to pollinizers. Unless it's a self-fertile cherry, you need two different cherries. This guy comes in who wants two Rainer cherries.

"No, you need two *different* cherries."

"But you said *two* cherries!"

"But they can't fertilize themselves."

"But they *are* two different cherries. One here and one there."

"You can't have the same variety. They're clones. They need a different variety of cherry."

"Why didn't you say so in the first place?"

A guy orders sod and a bag of 'starter' fertilizer. Just before his delivery, he calls, "Say, where is my topsoil?"

"Topsoil? What do you mean?"

"I'm supposed to get topsoil with my order."

"The sod has some soil. Is that what you mean?"

"No. I thought top soil came with the order."

"No. Just sod. Sorry. We have bags of topsoil if you want that."

"But I need a truckload."

"We don't sell bulk soil. There are a couple guys down the street who do that."

"But your flier says it comes with rich Delta peat soil."

"Yeah, that's the soil the grass grows in."

"Seems pretty misleading." (He hangs up.)

A lady tells me that her zucchini isn't forming the fruit properly. The fruit is just shriveling up.

"That's usually a pollination problem. You can always get the pollen from the male flower and with a little brush and dab it on the female flower."

"Male and female flowers? How can I tell which is which?"

I draw a picture of male and female flowers and explain how they are different.

"So, I can get any pollen from any plant and pollinate the zucchini? That's good to know."

"No. It has to be from the male zucchini flower."

"Why is that?"

"For the same reason you can't cross dogs and cats with each other."

"There is just so much to know!"

Lady insists that she needs organic pest control in her garden to kill ants.

"I'm disabled because of household chemicals that poisoned me. I can't be too careful."

"Yes, especially with things you have to eat."

"You are so right. I put dog flea collars in all of my food cabinets to keep any bugs out. I've been doing that for 20 years."

Lady comes in for a recommendation for a landscaper.

"Sure. We have quite a few landscapers."

"Great. I'd really like one that lets me do all the planting."

"I understand you have frost cloth? I need about fifty feet."

"Sure. What are you trying to protect?"

"I need to cover the ground to protect my daffodils and tulips."

"They are in the ground. That's enough protection. They don't need anything."

"That's okay. It will make me feel better."

"I need some frost cloth to cover my fruit trees."

"What do you have? Citrus or avocado?"

"No. Fruit trees. You know. Apples, peaches, and stuff."

"You don't need to cover those. They drop their leaves in the winter and go dormant. They need the cold to help them set fruit."

"They do?"

Lady buys an Early Elberta Peach tree.

"I notice that your label says "Self-Fertile." Please tell me what that means? Is it fertilized when first put in the ground, or what? I need to know if I should fertilize as I normally do with my other fruit trees."

A new Agricultural Inspector is inspecting each plant from a shipment we received, looking for Glassy-winged Sharpshooters. He is putting a small green inspection label on each pot that he inspects.

"Usually you inspect the whole shipment and put one inspection label on the paperwork," I explain.

"Oh, is that how it works? I was wondering about that."

A particularly needy lady who has been asking numerous questions, finally asked me about getting some potting soil.

"How much is the bag?"

"$5.99."

"No. How big is the bag?" she asked again.

"It's about so big," I answered spreading my hands.

"No," she replied, slightly frustrated. "How much is *in* the bag?"

"Oh, well, it's two cubic feet."

She heaved a frustrated sigh. "Thank you."

A lady is complaining about Monsanto and GMOs.

"How do you know that your vegetable plants are not GMO?" she complained.

"Because we've asked the company we buy from. They don't use any GMO seeds."

"How do you know they're not lying?"

"Why would they lie?"

"Why does Monsanto poison us with chemtrails in the sky?"

"Those aren't chemtrails. That is just water vapor. It's called contrails."

"I know they are poisoning us. After it rains, you can see bubbly stuff on the concrete. It's that poison from the airplanes."

"I have a rose that mutated!" a lady exclaimed.

"Mutated?"

"Yes! It was white and now it's pink! And the flower is totally different. It's amazing!"

"That's probably just the root stock. You get suckers that can take over the plant if you don't cut them out."

"It didn't mutate?"

"No. Sorry."

"Darn."

"I want lots of flowers in my yard, but I don't want any bees. What do you have?" asked a lady, frowning. "I am allergic to bees."

"Insects and bees are attracted to flowers. That's sort of the whole point of having flowers.

The plant gives them nectar and pollen, and the bees and other insects pollinate the plants."

"I know that bees like flowers, but aren't there some flowers that don't like bees?"

Lady wants a weed killer. She is holding a bottle of Roundup.

"The Bermuda grass is growing all over the place in my landscape," she explains.

"You have to be careful when spraying around your plants. Don't let the weed killer touch them."

"What difference does that make? I just want to kill the weeds. Doesn't weed killer just kill weeds?"

"Well, no. It will kill most plants if the spray gets on them," I tell her.

"Fine," she replied. "I'll just go to Lowe's. I'm sure they will have weed killer."

Are Tomatoes in Yet?

January 7: "Do you have any eggplant or tomato plants yet?" (The winner!)

January 8: "So, do you have tomato plants yet?"

January 15: Do you have any tomatoes yet?

January 28: "Do you have any tomatoes?"
"No, but we do have broccoli, lettuce, chard, and spinach. Stuff like that."
"There are other vegetables you can get besides tomatoes?"

February 1: "Do you have tomatoes? Mine died. Do I have to replant them every year?"

"It's too early for tomato plants. And, yeah, you have to replant them. The frost will kill them unless you have a greenhouse."

"They don't live year-round?"

What's the Matter with My Plant?

A customer brings in a branch of a Liquidambar tree.

"This Liquidambar tree you sold us is diseased. See all this weird growth on the branch? I say we should just cut it down. My *husband* wants to see what *you* think, first."

"That growth is normal. Liquidamber usually get that corky growth on the branches."

She frowns at her husband. He just smiles back.

A lady comes in with an Aucuba plant.

"What's wrong with my plant? I sprayed it with baking soda and water for mildew. That didn't work. What else should I do?"

"You don't have mildew. That fuzzy stuff is Cottony Cushion scale. It's an insect."

"An insect! Eww, gross! How did it get on there?"

"You know, I've never figured that out yet, but we can kill it."

"Thank goodness!"

A man and his wife come in with a branch of an African Sumac. It's turning yellow and they were wondering why. They seem to be doing everything right as far as watering and fertilizing. He mentions offhand that it suckers a lot, too.

"We have a product called Sucker Punch. You just cut them down and dab it with a brush. It will help stop the suckering."

"There are too many suckers. I just spray them with Roundup."

"But the suckers will absorb the roundup and go into the tree!"

His wife stares at him. "Maybe that's why it's turning yellow, dummy."

A customer and his wife come into the store with a branch of a peach tree. Half of the branch seems affected. The other half is fine. It looked like a chemical burn or spray drift. The newer leaves were wilted and shriveled. I asked him if he had sprayed anything, or maybe the neighbors did? The tree was far from the neighbors, and he hadn't sprayed anything at all. I said it wasn't a disease. Had he done *anything* near the tree? Anything at all?

"Oh, wait a second. I did build a fire and it was really hot."

"How far from the tree was the fire?"

"Oh, about ten feet."

"Well, there's your 'burn'."

"Wow," he said. "I never even thought of that."

His wife rolled her eyes.

An Agricultural Inspector frowns and shows me a fern frond.

"What is that stuff on the bottom of those fern leaves?"

"That's where the spores come from."

"What's the matter with my Star Jasmine? It gets all these weird white spots all over it after I trim it with my hedge trimmer. Is it a disease? Should I spray it with something?"

"No. When you cut a Star Jasmine, the saps leak out and drips. It's just sap. After you trim, just spray it with a hose right before it dries. It will wash all the white away."

"Really?" she asks me skeptically.

I grab a Star Jasmine and cut a branch. Immediately it starts to leak sap.

"Well, I'll be."

Customer tells me that her oak trees aren't doing well. The leaves are falling off and parts of the trees never got leaves. What could be wrong with it? I ask her to send me some pictures of the leaves and the trees. She never gets around to it. Instead, she hires an arborist to come out and tell her what is wrong. It turns out that her husband put about two feet of soil around the oaks when he was grading the property. The arborist suggests they clear out the soil around the oaks. She emails me some pictures of the oaks with a couple of feet of soil removed around the trunks. The soil stain on the bark is obvious.

"Do you think the arborist was right? Could that kill the oaks?"

"Absolutely that could kill the oaks. It usually takes about eight to ten years to kill the oaks, though. How long ago did he do that?"

"Eight years ago. Do you have something I could use to save them?"

Email conversation from customer: About a year ago, I bought ten Italian Cypress from you. Basically, they've done well. I went to make sure the auto-water was working well today, and on only one of them, it looks like the trunk is covered in SNAILS. It is not snails. though. Do you know what this is, and what I can do about it? I did some research and I think it is canker or something. Maybe I should pull the tree out and treat the ground before I plant another one?

Me: Perhaps it is scale. Without a picture, I can't be sure. Can you scrape them off? Smash them? Why don't you Google "scale" and look at the pictures. We also have systemic insecticides that you can use that are absorbed by the roots and protects the entire tree. I would also check all the other trees and make sure you don't have any on them.

Customer: Here is a picture of the affected tree. It is very firmly attached and about the size of a walnut. It seems to be the only tree affected. Interesting enough, it is the smallest tree, leading me to think that is has been affected for quite a while and maybe its growth has been stunted.

Me: Those are cypress cones. It's normal. If you don't like them, just cut them off.

A guy brings in a branch of a cherry with red bumps at the base of each leaf. What kind of disease is on it, he wonders? Is it insect eggs? What should he spray? he asks.

"It's just glands. It's normal. You don't have to do anything. All cherries have this."

"Are you sure? It looks pretty weird."

"It's normal. They're supposed to look like that."

"Okay, if you say so."

Guy brings in a rose branch in mid-January. It has no leaves.

"What's wrong with this rose? It started doing this a few weeks ago."

A lady calls the nursery. Her lemon tree is doing poorly.

"It dropped four leaves! They turned yellow and fell off! Am I overwatering it?"

"How often do you water it?" Jenny asked.

"Almost every day. It depends. I check with my moisture meter daily."

"That sounds okay. Have you fertilized it?"

"I'm afraid to fertilize it. What if I over-fertilize it?"

"You can always give it a half rate," Jenny suggested.

"But I have it in a pot. I'm just not sure what to do. If it gets too hot, I roll it into the house. When it cools down, I roll it back outside."

"You don't have to do that. Our citrus trees are out in the sun all day. They can take it."

"Really?" she asked. "I just want to be a good mom to my tree."

"You sound more like a helicopter mom. Just relax."

She laughed. "I suppose you're right."

Young guy comes in. He's having problems growing his cannabis plant. He bought five live goldfish and put them under the plant like the Indians were known to do. The plant is dying and turning black on the edges, and it smells funny.

"Do you think it needs some phosphorous?"

A lady comes in to talk to us about her crape myrtle. It's early spring and they are still dormant.

"My husband keeps ripping up our crape myrtle and throwing it on the compost pile. He says it's dead. I keep going out and saving it. How can I convince him it's still alive?"

"Crape myrtles always leaf out late. Just get your fingernail and scratch a small branch. It should be green underneath it. If the branch snaps off, or if it's brown when you scratch it, it's dead." I take her to one of our crape myrtles and show her what I mean.

"Great. I'll do that when I get home."

She calls back an hour later.

"I was right! It's still alive. He promised not to rip it out again. Thanks so much!"

Interesting Customers

I answer the phone. "Rising Sun Nursery. Can I help you?"

"Do you carry Euphrates Poplars?"

"No, sorry. We only carry Cotton-less Cottonwoods. Those are poplars also."

"I really need the Euphrates Poplar. They were used in ceremonies from Babylon."

"You can't use a substitute? Some other poplar?"

"No. It really needs to be a Euphrates Poplar. Can you get them at big wholesale nurseries?"

"Not likely," I said. "If I have never heard of it, then it's not likely they will have them."

"I really need that particular poplar to make magic. Years ago, I did magic and kind of screwed myself up doing it. I need to follow the recipe exactly this time. Man, I tell you it really works."

"Maybe you can find it online somewhere," I told him. "It's not even in the *Western Garden* book. You're not going to find it around here anywhere."

"Hey, well thanks for your time."

"Sure. Good luck."

A lady bought five pairs of clippers.

"Why so many clippers?"

"I hate to sharpen them. This way, when one pair gets dull, I can just use a new one."

Diamond, our store cat, was meowing and being a nuisance. She wanted a treat. Susan, who was at the register, says, "Sorry, cat, you're just going to have to wait."

The customer waiting says, "Are you talking to me?"

Turns out the customer's name was Cat.

A lady comes in with her husband and explains that she needs to replace a lot of her plants in their landscape because she was preoccupied with her son's trial for murder. Her aunt was supposed to take care of the landscape during her son's trial.

"Yeah," her husband snickered. "But she killed them all."

A lady brought some tomato plants, some fertilizer, and a Bird's Nest fern up to the counter. While there, she handed me some literature about the Rapture, also known as the "End Times" that was coming up in two weeks.

"You and your employees might want to read this," she said with a knowing look.

A lady with wild curly red hair told me that she needs to wear a helmet when she gardens. She was attacked by a hawk that knocked her down. At first, she thought maybe she was shot by a crazy neighbor and was going to call the police. Then the bird attacked again.

"Now I wear a helmet, and I don't have any more problems."

Guy buys a shovel, hoe, hose, a bag of potting soil, and a couple of tomato plants. He came in with a motorcycle and doesn't own anything else to drive. I was wondering how he was going to load all of this on the motorcycle.

"How are you going to take this home?"

"I'm not. I need you to deliver it."

Customer calls on the phone: "I'm worried about my peach trees. I think they are stressed."

Susan discussed proper watering and fertilizing her trees. The lady tells her what she is doing.

Susan: "Well, it sounds like you are doing everything right."

Customer: "Right? Right? (She bursts into tears.) I fell asleep and when I woke up my son was dead. Why? Why did it have to happen?"

Susan: "I am so sorry. I will pray for you."

Customer: (Suddenly quite calm) "Honey, lots of people *say* that. I'll tell you right now. It doesn't do any good." (She hangs up.)

An odd couple came in boasting about how they compost everything. "We even compost our underwear!" she chirped.

A guy comes in always driving his brother's classic car.
"Wow! That's a nice car!"
"Yeah, it's my brother's car."
"Can I help you?"
"Yeah, my brother needs some plants for his house."
(At least that is what he tells us. And when he comes in, he's always driving his brother's car and says he's buying plants for his brother. Does he have a brother? In the couple of years that he came in, we never did see his brother.)

Walt, an old guy in his mid-to-late seventies or early eighties, was by far the most outlandish and craziest customer we ever had. His long-suffering wife would just sit in the car and wait for his antics to wind down. He claimed she waited in the car because she had Alzheimer's. But when he needed money, he had to go see her first.

Walt had a story for everything. This time he was in rare form. In fact, he was so nutty that he was entertaining. What could he possibly come up with next?

Walt went on about how he caught fifteen fish in thirty minutes. He said he would bring me some. He could make his own beer—fifty gallons in just three minutes. Just add water.

"Did it have any alcohol in it?" Walt usually ignored my questions, he was too wrapped up in his stories.

Walt had hundreds of boats. He was a billionaire. He owned fifty jeeps. He found four hundred crab cages along the beach. He found a 575-pound anchor on the beach too. He had to get help to drag it ashore. He still had it. While he was there, he found twenty-five pieces of gold that had been imbedded in the sand for fifty years. Walt grinned. "You think I'm shitting you. It's all true!"

He found a bottle that was filled with wine. It was three thousand years old. He asked me what I thought it was worth.

"I don't think you could calculate it."

Then he said he found a chair on the beach from the Titanic. It floated ashore in perfect condition.

"Did you find it in the Atlantic or the Pacific Ocean?" I asked, not expecting an answer.

About this time, I was getting tired of Walt and was trying to leave the gift shop. A customer came in with a flat of vegetables and said he had a question about tomatoes.

"I'm an expert on tomatoes!" Walt said, beaming.

"Well, maybe I should ask you, then," stated the unsuspecting customer.

I quickly slipped away. Walt, though, was in his glory. He followed the customer into the store and all the way into the parking lot. The customer got into his car and tried to get away, but Walt was walking along and leaning on the car while talking to the customer through his open window, spouting more advice. Finally, the customer pleaded that he had to go. He sped off.

Walt, his cup finally filled, got in his car and drove off too.

"Was that guy off his medication?" Judy asked.

"I don't think he takes any medication," I answered. "But he just drove away."

Judy stared at me. "You mean he was driving?!"

Sadly, Walt's visits finally came to an end. No more wild and crazy stories about Indian burial grounds under his house. No more clanging the gift store chimes if nobody was paying attention to him. His last visit he could barely walk. His health was deteriorating rapidly. No more stuffing his little PT Cruiser with plants and bags of manure. One of my employees asked me why I bothered with the old coot. I explained that someday, I was going to write a book, and Walt was going to be in it.

That Costs Too Much!

The phone rings. "Rising Sun Nursery. Can I help you?"

"Yes. I need some dirt for some pots," a man stated. "What should I do?"

"Dirt? As in potting soil?" I asked.

"No. You know. Some dirt that I can mix with peat moss or something."

"You want to dig it up on your property?"

"No. Down there at your place."

"We don't do anything like that, but we do have potting soil."

"Buy it? Don't you have some dirt down there that I can get?"

"We have potting soil in bags."

"But this is for five 15-gallon pots."

"One bag should fill each pot. They cost 5.99 each."

"But that would cost $30 to fill them up!"

"Well, you could buy half a yard of planter mix in bulk down the street if you have a pickup. That runs about $35 but you could get a lot more for your money."

"$35! The whole world is going crazy! Hell, I'll just go dig it up alongside the road. Just forget it!" (He hangs up.)

A lady ordered two flats of African Daisy—one with white flowers and one with purple flowers. I quoted her $10 per flat. When they came in, we called her, and she came down to the nursery. She complained repeatedly about the price of the plants, the cost of fuel, and her hairdresser.

"I can't possibly afford to buy *both* flats. Couldn't I get like a half-flat of each?"

She left in a brand-new SUV.

Older guy comes in to buy a couple six-packs of tomatoes. We charge him $2.59 for each pack. He complains.

"I thought these were $2.49!"

"They went up ten cents."

"Oh, that makes me so angry. I'm never coming back here." He stomps out.

A guy bought a bundle of fifty red onion plants for $3.99. He complained that the price was *way* too high. "I don't even want to look at the receipt," He griped. "It makes me so mad."

A customer named Nick would call every couple of weeks and complain that our tomato six-packs were too high.

"You know, your six-packs cost twenty cents more than at CVS."

An older guy comes in. He has over thirty roses to spray. I show him the granular systemic insecticide, but he buys a liquid concentrate instead. I show him our most inexpensive one-gallon sprayer.

"$18.99?! Your sprayers are too expensive. What else do you have?"

"We have these little spray bottles for $2.49."

"Perfect. I'll get that."

"Your hand is going to get tired. It will take you forever to sprays all those roses."

"That's okay. It will work. I can't afford to pay big bucks for a sprayer."

Can I Get a Deal?

Guy buys two one-gallon Trumpet Vines.
"Will you give me a deal if I buy two more? I like to dicker."

We had some Photinia one-gallon priced at $6.99.
"Can I get these for $5 if I buy four?" a lady asks.

Lady calls me over to our chimes display.
"Will you take 50 percent off one of the large chimes here?"
"No."
"How about 20 percent?"
"No."
"10 percent?"
"How about zero percent off? They just came in a couple weeks ago."

It was the end of the season and we had a bunch of extra heirloom tomatoes in four-inch pots. We were giving away two heirloom tomatoes with any purchase. A lady put three six-packs and six heirloom tomatoes on the counter figuring she got two tomatoes with each six-pack.

"No. You only get two with your purchase."

"What if I pay for each six-pack separately? That will be three purchases."

"No. There is a limit of two per customer."

"Where does it say that on the sign?"

"Right here." I get a marker and write it on the sign.

We have a plastic insert normally filled with flyers about Heirloom tomatoes and their descriptions, but currently it is empty. On the front of the display is a "Take One" sign. Next to that is a sign that says "Heirloom Tomatoes. $1.99 each". A lady took one Heirloom tomato.

"The sign said, 'Take One' so I thought they were free."

We have a sale on planter mix. 'Buy 3, get 1 Free!' Many customers argue with us that if they buy two, they should get the third bag free. I explain that it says, "Buy 3", not buy two. We finally change our sign and ask the vendor to change their sign to 'Buy 3, get the 4th bag Free!' The arguments finally stop.

"What kind of deal can I get if I buy three trees?" (This gets asked a lot. It's like the third tree or bush crosses a red line and an instant discount should kick in.)

"We give a 5 percent discount if you buy ten of any one thing."

"Ten? I don't need that much. Never mind."

"Do I get a discount if I'm a contractor?"

"What kind of contractor are you? A landscape contractor?"

"No, I'm a plumber, but sometimes I fix up houses and sell them."

"That's nice, but we only do discounts for people actually in the landscaping business."

"Is the owner here?"

"I'm the owner." (Uh-oh. I know what's coming.)

"I'm landscaping my house. I need at least three trees and about five shrubs. Do you give discounts?"

"You have to get at least ten of something of the same variety to get a discount of five percent. It goes up to ten percent if you get twenty and so forth."

"That's all? Why so stingy?"

"Do they give you a discount at Home Depot or Lowes if you buy a few plants?"

"Well, no. But then the owner isn't there. I thought maybe you'd want my business."

(He walks out.)

Angry Customers

A guy calls us about a plant. Judy can't figure out what particular plant he is talking about.

"Look, you guys called *us*. Now you don't know what we're talking about? What kind of crappy business is this? How *incompetent* can you get?"

"I'm sorry. I don't seem to have your names on any paperwork."

"Well, I have paperwork. Right here. You called us yesterday. It says Joe from Pine Grove Nursery called us at 3 pm."

"But this is Rising Sun Nursery. We don't have anybody named Joe here."

"What nursery is this?"

"Rising Sun Nursery."

"Oops. Sorry. Wrong nursery." (They hang up.)

A lady was very concerned about GMOs. "Monsanto is out to get us. And if I find out that you have any vegetables altered in any way, I'm coming back here!"

People come in five minutes to closing. They grab a cart and then start arguing about which trees to get. They can't decide.

"You know, we are open seven days a week from 9 to 5."

"Oh, you're making us leave? Fine. Let's get out of here." They stomp off in a huff.

A woman comes in with a rose tree in late May. The roots are in a bag and it has no leaves. I take the rose and look at it.

"I bought this rose here in January, and it never leafed out," she states testily.

"This has a Jackson-Perkins label. We don't sell Jackson-Perkins roses, just Weeks roses. Plus, Angel Face isn't one I normally carry because it seems more susceptible to mildew."

"I know where I bought the rose! Are you saying you are not going to stand behind your plants?"

"We do. When the plants come from us. Do you have a receipt?"

"A receipt?!" she says, her voice rising in pitch. "I'm telling you I bought this rose here! Where else would I buy it?"

"Let me look at the rose." I inspect it. The stems are green and plump. It looks like it will survive. "Okay, I'll give you credit for this, but we still don't carry Jackson-Perkins roses."

She leaves satisfied, and now I have a leafless rose tree. I buried it completely in sand and water it every day. The warm days and moisture start working their magic. It's called 'sweating.' In a week it starts budding out. I take it out of the sand, pot it up, put it in the shade house for a couple weeks, and then place it out in the sun. A couple months later, a lady sniffed the rose, admired the lavender flowers, bought the rose, and took it home.

I can't say anymore that I *don't* sell Jackson-Perkins roses.

A guy calls and claims that we sold him a maple tree last year when he really wanted a liquidambar tree. I ask him to bring in a leaf, so we can identify it. He digs up the whole tree in the middle of August and brings it in just before closing with no pot and its roots exposed. It is a large Trident Maple in bad shape. He's in a big hurry, so he just leaves it with us and doesn't leave his phone number. We put it in a pot and place it in the shade house. After a couple weeks, it is obviously dead, so we throw it in the dump pile.

He comes in a week later and wants his tree.

"You had *no* right to dump my tree! It was perfectly fine when I brought it in here."

"Actually, it was dead. You can't dig a tree up in the middle of August and bring it in without a pot."

"You said to bring in the tree."

"I said to bring in a *leaf* so I could I.D. it, not the whole tree!"

"Fine. Don't expect me to ever shop at your store again!"

Returns

A lady bought some of our good organic potting soil. While we were loading it, she noticed that one of the ingredients was bat guano.

"I'm sorry. I need to return that. It has bat poop in it, and my kids will eat it."

"I need to return this bottle of insecticide. It won't work for me."

"Oh? What are you trying to kill?"

"I have yellow caterpillars and as you can see, this caterpillar on the front of the bottle is green. I need something that kills yellow caterpillars. What do you have?"

A guy in a cowboy hat and boots and a big western belt buckle saunters in and buys a house plant to give to his girlfriend. He brought it back all dried up after a few weeks.

"It's all dried up. Did you water it?"

"Nobody told me I had to do that."

A lady came back to the store in early April with her damaged tomato plant.

"My tomato got some disease. The leaves have all these holes in it. I want a new one."

"Yeah, that's from hail. See all the holes where the hail hit it?"

"Oh? I never thought of that. We *did* have hail the other day."

"That's right."

"Well?" she asked.

"Well what?"

"Are you going to replace it?"

"I am returning this plant because it has bug eggs in the soil."

"Bug eggs?"

"Yes. Can I get a different one, please?"

"Let me look at it." I observe the plant. "Those aren't bug eggs. Those are slow-release fertilizer pellets."

"Are you saying you're not going to give me a new plant?"

A couple brings back a dried-up maple after a week and immediately demand that they receive a new tree, or they are never going to shop at our store again. The tree is bone dry and the leaves are fried.

"Did you ever water it? The soil is completely dry."

"It rained last week," the man answers defensively.

"It's June. You have to water this tree daily. The temperature has been close to 90 almost every day."

The woman is furious. "Are you going to give us a credit on this tree or not?"

"No," I answer. "Not if you don't water the tree."

"Fine! Come on, Ralph, let's go." She stomps off.

Meanwhile, I examine the small branches. The leaves are burned but the small branches are not shriveled up and look plump enough to survive. I get a hose and start watering it, figuring maybe I can bring it back.

"Stop watering it!" she screams at me. "We're taking the tree with us! Ralph, get the tree."

I hand the dripping tree back to him.

"Do you want some plastic?" I offer.

Another customer, watching the scene play out, rips off a sheet of plastic and hands it to the man as he heads out of the nursery. He shakes his head. "Wow. You get some real doozies in here."

A guy pulls up in a pickup. There is a dead-looking tree in the back.

"I bought this fruit tree here last year. It died recently. Do you have a return policy? I did

everything right, but it just died."

"Let me look at it." I notice some borer damage on the trunk. "You got borers at some point.

See the sawdust and sort of engraving on the trunk? That's borers."

"I never noticed that. What do they look like?"

"Hang on." I grab the tree and lean it up against a cart and step on it, cracking the tree in half.

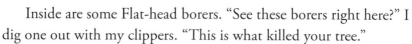

Inside are some Flat-head borers. "See these borers right here?" I dig one out with my clippers. "This is what killed your tree."

"Well, I'll be."

"They hide inside the tree until they're ready to come out. They lay eggs on the tree, especially if the tree gets damaged by sunburn like this one was. I bet this sunburn here was on the southwest side of the tree."

"Now that you mention it, that *was* on the southwest side of the tree. How did you know that?"

"Trees are just like people. If you don't get enough water, they overheat. The hottest side is the southwest side. You can whitewash it with white latex paint, and it will keep it cooler. Plus, mulching it will keep the roots moister and less stressed."

"I came in here feeling cheated that my tree died. Instead, I see the mistakes I made, and now I want to get some more fruit trees and do it right. I appreciate it."

"You're quite welcome."

"I'm afraid I'm going to have to return these one-gallon roses." A lady sets three ground cover roses in a box on the counter. On inspection, they seem fine.

"Why? What's wrong with them?"

"They have thorns. I didn't know roses were going to have thorns."

Unanswerable Questions

A lady wanted to know how she got fruit on her fruit tree because she insisted that it didn't bloom this year.

"It had to have bloomed. That's the only way trees get fruit."

"No, I'm telling you. It didn't get one blossom. It's a real mystery. How did it do that?"

Customer wants some planting mix.

"But I want some with no amendments in it. Do you have that?"

I write a funny story ("The Tree Sale") about giving away some talking trees and send it out in a monthly newsletter.

A guy comes in to the nursery and looks around. "Where are the free trees?"

"Free trees?"

"Yeah, you had in your newsletter that you were giving away free trees."

"That was just a story. There are no free trees."

"Huh," he responds, and walks out.

A man was interested in buying four hundred Thuya bushes. "Can you find any crossed with birch? I understand it makes them hardier." (I still haven't found any.)

Email: "How do you kill frogs? There are hundreds of mini-frogs that adorn our house and garden, walls, and waterfalls. They make such a mess all over the outside doors and walls, not to mention are becoming house pets as well. The cats are only interested in gophers and mice." (You really want to kill those cute little frogs? All that poop is from eating bugs!)

Lady calls in about morning glory growing on the grave where her cat, Vanilla, is buried.
"It's growing over his head. I want to get rid of it, but I don't want to use poison on my cat. What should I do?"

"What kind of nitrogen will make my cherries self-fruitful?"

Email: We are going to move the Japanese maple tree as per the attached to a friend's house. Please let me know if it would hurt to cut each branch so it is not much wider than the tree. Thank you, Harold.

Lady brought in a branch each of her two clematis vines.
"Can you tell the difference and the color of the flower? I mixed up the labels and I'm not sure which one is which anymore." (I'm good, but not *that* good.)

"Mushrooms are coming up in my landscape. Can I eat them, Don? What do you think?"

Another hungry customer asks, "How can I tell if plants are poisonous? Is there a way? How can I tell if I can just eat them?"

"I would like to plant some trees and bushes. Can you help me?"
"How big is your area?"
"It's about as big as my living room."

A guy insisted that his blueberry was growing like crazy. It was getting quite big.
"Is it normal for a blueberry to get that big?"
"Bring in a piece of it in to show me."
Later that day, he brought in a willow branch.
"That willow was a weed that came up in your blueberry plant. That's not a blueberry."
"No, it is. I picked blueberries directly from this plant. How is that possible if it's not a blueberry?"

A lady comes into the store with a faded plastic snake and wants to know what color it was supposed to be. It was a bleached flesh tone but still had some dark bands on it.
"I don't know. Brown?"
"Yes, but what kind of brown? I bought it here. I thought you'd know."
"We've never sold a snake like that before."
"Well, how would you know? Who does your buying?" She looks around for a woman.
"I do."
"*You* do?" She looks at me skeptically and then sees Denise. "Do you know what color this snake should be?"
Denise looks at it. "I don't know. Brown?"
"I bought it here. Doesn't anyone know?"
"I've been here seven years and I don't remember a snake like that," Denise replies.
"Fine. How am I supposed to know what color to paint it?"

"We do have a book on animals. It has pictures of snakes in it."

"Oh, that would be wonderful!"

Unfortunately, she can't find one picture that looks like her snake. On her way out, she spots Judy coming in from watering.

"Do you know the coloring should be on this snake?"

"I don't know. Brown?"

Answerable but Silly Questions

"Do you sell grass?"

"You mean sod? Yes, but you have to order it."

"Will it be green?"

"Yes."

"What color is Kentucky Bluegrass then?"

"Green."

"Why do they call it "bluegrass" then?"

"When the grass blooms, it looks blue. It's always mowed so it looks green."

"Grass blooms?"

A customer asked what onions look like after you grow them. I suggested he look in the grocery store. "I know," he said. "But are yours different?"

Guy has a bottle of Bayer 2'n 1, which is a combination of fertilizer and systemic insect killer. "How long does it take for the aphids to kill the rose bush?"

"You mean, how long to kill the aphids? About three to four days."

"No, to kill the rose!"

"Aphids won't kill your rose."

"Really?"

"Trust me."

A lady calls on the phone and wants to know the exact size of a roll of sod.

"They are two feet by five feet," Denise tells her.

"No. How tall is the roll?"

"How tall? What do you mean?"

Clearly irate now, the lady says, "When it's rolled up. How high is the roll?"

"I'm sorry. I don't exactly know. Maybe you can talk to the owner?"

"Can't someone answer the question?"

Denise motions me to come to the phone. "This lady wants to know the size of a roll, rolled up. I'm not sure."

"Hello. This is Don. Can I help you?"

"Can't anyone tell me the size of a roll of sod at your nursery?"

"Sure. It's two feet wide by five feet long and maybe a foot high or less rolled up. Why do you need to know that?"

"I just want to be sure that I can fit two rolls in the back of my pickup truck."

We were selling pendulums in the gift shop. "How do you get them to work?" a lady asked.

"Do you have anything we can haul plants around in?"

"Yes. Those blue carts over there."

The customer looks over to see a dozen blue carts lined up near the entrance.

"Oh, I thought those were just for employees."

"How do you get rid of frogs? We have a pond, and the frogs are too noisy."

A lady has a question about male and female kiwis.

"Which one gets the fruit?" (Do I really need to explain this one?)

A lady claims that she has aphids in her carpets.

"Are you sure they're not fleas?"

"Fleas?! My pets don't have fleas. No, they're aphids. What can I use to get rid of them?"

Guy brings some nice black olives in a bag that he just picked from his tree.

"There must be something wrong with them. They're ripe but they taste terrible."

Guy comes in with a branch of a Coyote Bush.

"What's eating my oak trees? They never get any taller than me."

"This is a Coyote Bush, not an oak tree."

"How can you be so sure?"

"See these flowers? Oaks don't get flowers like this. And oaks get acorns."

"I was wondering about that."

Guy came in with his wife. He wanted to know why he had foam in his pond.

"Could any soap have gotten into your pond?" I asked.

"Well, we add reclaimed water from the washing machine."

"I think that's your problem."

His wife glared at him. "I *told* you so!"

Note left for me: On a fruitless mulberry, what is the variety it is grafted to that makes it a "fruitless" tree? (The rootstock has nothing to do with it being fruitless. A fruitless Mulberry is a male tree grafted onto a seedling mulberry rootstock.)

Lady called in the middle of winter and wondered why the ornamental plums in front of CVS Pharmacy didn't have any leaves. "Are they dead?" she asked. "The people there didn't know. They couldn't tell me."

"It is winter. They are just dormant."

"Trees go dormant in the winter? Really?"

"Yes. Many trees lose their leaves in the winter."

"I had no idea."

Lady has a crabgrass lawn and wants to keep it just the way it is. "No, I don't want to kill the crabgrass. I like it. I want a weed killer to get rid of the rest of the weeds though. Any suggestions?"

A guy wants something to stop the frogs from eating his hydrangeas. He says they are leaving little holes in the leaves.

"What can I do to get rid of those damn frogs?"

"I don't know how to get rid of frogs, but they didn't make those holes."

"Now what else would be doing it? Those frogs are all over them."

"How am I supposed to know when to put netting on my tree to protect the fruit? There are no instructions."

Richard, an occasional customer, was interested in some ceramic pots. Except he refused to buy any pots from China. He wanted to buy pots from Italy or the U.S.A. only. He suggested that we check into it.

"Aren't there other people who feel the way I do about this?"

A lady was moving to Valley Springs, near the nursery, and bringing her houseplants with her. "Will my houseplants do okay in your area?"

Customer called on the phone. "Do you have any houseplants that will grow in Fresno?"

A lady was buying a grapevine that had grapes on it. She wanted to know when the next crop of grapes would happen.

"They will get grapes next year."

"You mean they only fruit once a year? Really?"

We posted a sign: 'Strawberries: 1 gal. only $3.99 each'

A lady asks, "Does that mean I can only take one?"

Lady is happy that the potting soil has worms in it. I explain that worm castings are just worm poop—not worms. They separate the castings from the worms.

"What? No worms at all?"

"Which is softer, a lilac or a hibiscus?" asked a lady.

"Softer? What do you mean?"

"I need to know in case my grandson has to jump out the window if there is a fire."

"What plants have spines that don't get too big?"

"Barberry 'Crimson Pygmy' with the red leaves don't get too big."

"If I planted barberry under my daughter's window, would it keep her from getting out?"

Email: Do you have any Rising Sun Fuji Apple trees for sale? If so, how tall are they and what is the price? Thanks, Ralph.

Me: We have lots of Fuji apples. They are about six feet tall and cost $39.99.

Ralph: Not just Fuji. They are called Rising Sun Fuji.

Me: I'm sorry. I never heard of Rising Sun Fuji apples. But I looked it up and there is such a thing. I thought you meant the trees at our nursery. I thought you wanted a Rising Sun Nursery Fuji apple tree.

Lady brings a bag of dried-up leaves in a paper bag.

"Can you identify these leaves? I meant to come last week but got delayed. You *can* identify them, right? I heard you were the best at doing that."

"Don't you have some spray that will kill *everything*?"

"Everything? Are talking about bugs or weeds?"

"Everything. Why do I have to have all these different bottles for things?"

"We have some broad-spectrum insecticides that kill most insects. And for weed control—"

"You don't understand. I want it for *everything*."

"Like a nuclear bomb?"

"Exactly!"

"How do you kill earthworms? They are like everywhere."

Guy comes into the nursery and looks around impatiently. "I'm looking for *hybrid* trees. Not the regular trees that you carry. Don't you have any *hybrid* trees?"

"My beans are coming up with their negative side up. What's going on?"

Phone call: "I have a question. How many plants are there in a six-pack?"

"So where will these branches end up as the tree grows and matures?" a lady asked, pointing to a maple tree she wanted to buy.

"Branches don't move. The tree doesn't stretch like a growing kid. They are set. If you want to raise the tree up, you have to prune the lower branches off. The tree gets more branches higher up as it grows."

"That's what I like about coming here. I always learn something new."

My daughter, Erin, was watering in the bedding plant area. A lady approached her carrying a couple bands of lemon cucumbers.

"Do these cucumbers really taste like a lemon?"

"No, they taste like a cucumber, but they're round."

"So why do they call them a lemon cucumber, then?"

"Because they turn yellow when they get older."

"No lemon taste at all?"

"Nope. Sorry."

The lady pointed. "And those sweet banana peppers?"

"Taste more like a sweet bell pepper."

"Got it."

Customer: "Can I plant these flowers by my front door?"

Guy says *he* wants to start a nursery like ours. "Your plants look nice. Do you ever fertilize them?" (If you need to ask if we fertilize, it might be better to forget starting a nursery.)

I delivered some trees to a realtor and he told me he wanted to start a nursery on some of his acreage. "I don't know much about plants really, so could you tell me what I should grow?" (Maybe you'd better stay in the real estate business.)

Did You Really Do That?

A guy called on the phone and had a question about a fruit tree that wasn't doing very well. He bought it from a big box store in a plastic bag and planted it.

"Should I have taken the bag off first before I planted it?"

A lady came into the store and said she drove away and forgot her potting soil the previous day. I told her to drive where the bagged goods were, and I would load them for her. She drove away without the potting soil—again.

A lady from Australia, new to the gardening world of California, bought a half dozen fruit trees from a catalog instead of her local nursery. (Okay, I had to rub that in.)

"The ground was very hard, but there were some nice soft mounds of soil in my yard, so I planted my fruit trees in the mounds. But something ate them." She held up a couple of fruit trees with the chewed roots.

"Those were gopher mounds. You fed those trees to the gophers."

"Really? What's a gopher? We don't have those in Australia."

(To be fair, she studied, headed up a garden for an elementary school, joined the Master Gardeners, and later became president of their local chapter.)

A guy wants some help tying two 15-gallon walnut trees to the top of his Suburban.

"Are you sure?"

"Oh yeah, I do this all the time."

A fellow comes into the store. He has a problem with his Japanese maple. The leaves are kind of dried up. The wine barrel doesn't seem to drain well anymore so he ripped up the tree and let the root ball dry out for a couple days. Then he got rooting hormone, added it to hot water, and soaked the roots in it. "What else can I do?"

The guy with the Japanese maple came back the next day. His moisture meter said his soil was moist, but the pH was "dead." He tested it, and it was dead.

"Your pH isn't "dead," it's probably just low."

"If I dump some dolomite lime in the pot, would it bring back my pH?"

"Well, technically yes, but what kind of potting soil are you using?"

"Oh, I don't do well with potting soil. It just grows weeds, so I threw it out."

"What are you using then?"

"I don't know, something called Tree & Shrub."

"What is that?"

"I don't know, but it's kind of chunky."

"Before you use dolomite, I suggest that you bring me a sample of your soil, or the bag."

"Sure, I can do that. Gee thanks!"

A customer asks Denise where the sage plants are. She points to the one-gallon section of ornamental sages. He walks over there, rips off a leaf, and starts chewing on it.

"I don't think any of those are edible."

"No?"

"You might want to head over to the herb section in the shade house."

I was sitting at home watching the Super Bowl with three minutes to go when the phone rings. Who could that be?

"I have some questions about azaleas. Can you help me?" Somehow, this guy got my home phone.

"There is only three minutes to go in the Superbowl!"

"I only have a *few* questions. It shouldn't take too long."

After half an hour of looking at our ornamental tile catalog, a woman got up with her notes.

"Thank you. I got all the information I need to go order it online."

Lady calls on the phone. "Do you have anybody who knows anything about walnuts?"

Jenny: "What kinds of questions do you have?"

Lady: There is a momentary pause. "Yeah. Right." (She hangs up.)

A local lady and her friend from Taiwan are visiting the nursery. They want to look at five-gallon fruiting cherry trees. They want to take them back to Taiwan. Which would be the best trees to take?

"But they are too big. How are you going to take them back?" I ask.

One of the ladies explains that she is going to wash all the soil off, cut them to about a foot tall, and stick them in her suitcase. We look through the trees and pick out some that have some little branches coming out near the base. I explain that suckers are from the root stock. They talk about the choices and then select two.

"Is this even legal? They let you bring plants like this into the country?"

Oh sure, they explain. They can't bring anything to California, but they bring things into Taiwan all the time.

"Do you want me to cut the trees for you?"

"No. We'll cut them when we get home to make sure they fit."

Denise was helping a guy at the counter. She gave him the total and he started to remove his pants. His pants dropped to the floor, revealing his shorts underneath.

"What do you think you're doing?"

He reached into his shorts pocket and pulled out his wallet.

"Oh, I have my wallet in my shorts. I was doing a lot of dirty work and didn't want to get my wallet dirty."

A lady on the phone asks tons of questions about fruit trees, pollination, fertilizers, varieties, and diseases. Finally, she says, "Thank you so much! See you in about a year!"

Lady said their almond trees had borers. "My husband slathered tar about half inch thick on the tree all the way up to the small branches. Do you think he killed them?"

"The trees or the borers?"

"I was told to put banana peels on the ground around my plants to get rid of aphids. And it really works! They're all gone." a lady exclaimed.

"What time of the year did you do that?" I asked. At the time it was early August.

"It was at the end of spring, in June sometime."

"You know, between beneficial insects and the heat, the aphids sort of naturally disappear in the summer. I never spray for aphids this time of year. I don't think the bananas did anything."

"No, no! Please don't pop my bubble!"

Lady calls on the phone.

"Rising Sun Nursery. Can I help you?"

"Yes. I'm here at Lowe's looking at chemicals. I'm confused. What should I spray for caterpillars?"

"There's nobody there to help you?"

"I suppose, but I know you know your stuff. That's why I'm calling you."

"We have chemicals at *our* nursery for that if you'd like to come visit us."

"Well, I just happened to be at Lowe's."

"We have organic as well as regular chemicals to use on caterpillars. I'm not really sure what they have at Lowe's."

"Well, I *suppose* I could come in and see what you have."

"That would be nice. Hope to see you soon."

A guy brings his mother into the store. They are both from an Eastern European country. She speaks no English. They wander around the nursery picking and eating fruit from the five-gallon trees. They dump some orange peels on the ground. She is stuffing her coat with fruit. I tell them to not pick the fruit because it is for the customers who want to buy the tree. They always want a deal on everything. They are exhausting.

"We buy these Pomegranate trees."

I notice the price stickers have been changed.

"You changed the prices."

"No, no. These are marked like this. We pay that price."

"I don't think so. I priced these myself." I have to draw the line on trying to steal from us. "I don't want you to come back here. You are not welcome. Please leave the store."

He translates for her. She makes some juicy comment, and they stomp out.

You Can't Do That

A lady came in with her boyfriend. She wanted to root her cut Noble Fir Christmas tree. She was worried because it was dropping needles. We told her to forget it. You can't root a cut Christmas tree.

"I'm going to try it anyway," her boyfriend said, and bought some rooting hormone. "My friend told me it could be done."

Guy planted his tree in a deep hole. He covered the root ball with six inches of soil over the base of the tree. It had been about a year now and the leaves slowly turned red and then black.

"What the heck is wrong with my tree?"

"You can't cover your trunk like that. That will kill it!"

"Well, nobody ever told me that."

"I need something to sterilize the ground. I have this bamboo I want to dig up and then sterilize the ground around it."

"I'm pretty sure that is a restricted chemical. We don't sell soil sterilizers. Maybe you should use brush killer first, kill the bamboo, and then dig it out."

"What? We have it back in Indiana. Are you telling me you can't get it?"

"This is California, and I can't get it."

"Well, in Indiana they sell it on the street corner. I'm sure if you tried harder, you could carry it. I don't want to do it *your* way, I want to do it *my* way."

Lots of people like a grove of birch trees. I spaced out three tall one-gallon pots in a 15-gallon pot to make a little grove. Now, after a year of growing and being trained, they were finally ready for sale. Soon a guy wanted to buy one.

"Can I divide these when I get home?"

"Why in the world would you want to do that? It's supposed to be a grove."

"It's cheaper than buying three five-gallon birch."

Don Urbanus

Don got his BS Degree (He loves to say that.) in Horticulture from Cal Poly, San Luis Obispo, in 1979. After college, he worked as a foreman at Boething Treeland, a large wholesale nursery in Northern California. In 1983, Don became the Production Manager for A to Z Tree Nursery, a wholesale/retail nursery in Los Gatos, and eventually moved to start his own wholesale nursery in Calaveras County on five acres in 1988, where he also designed and built his house. In 1997, he decided to get into retail by starting Rising Sun Nursery and renting a spot in Burson. Five years later, Don bought nine acres and moved down the street to its current location in 2002 and has been in business there ever since.

Rising Sun Nursery has won many awards as Best Nursery/ Garden Center in Calaveras and several times as Best Nursery in the Tri-County area. In 2013, Rising Sun Nursery was picked the Best Business in Calaveras County as well as the Best Nursery.

Don, a storyteller since childhood, has been writing short stories all his life, specializing in humorous tales. He wrote gardening articles and editorials for his local newspaper and stories for his nursery newsletter. Starting in 2000, for eighteen years, he participated in fundraiser melodramas for the local Friends of the Library—acting, singing, directing, and writing a dozen melodramas. In 2003, Don was chosen the Citizen of the Year by the Valley Springs Area Business Association.

This book is a compilation of a wandering mind, inspired by plants and people. Don is working on a mystery novel set in a nursery. There will be death, but not necessarily for the plants.

Contact Don at:
    don@donsnursery.com
    www.donsnursery.com

Erin Urbanus,
Illustrations & Cover Art

An artist since she could hold a pencil, Erin has always held a focus on art. Inspired by the many comics and fiction novels read growing up, the many beloved pets she has had over the years, and the lush nursery that was her childhood home, Erin puts this inspiration into her own work, both illustration and studio art. An alumnus of Humboldt State University with a BA in studio art, she operates as an independent artist and freelance illustrator on the northern California coast.

Contact Erin at:
erys.menagerie@gmail.com
erysstudio.com

More comments about "Darn Weeds!:

"Don is an amazing storyteller. If I didn't know better, I would've thought he made it all up."—**Erica Carnea**

"Don has an astonishing imagination. I've never seen anything like this book! But now, when I see him wandering around with his clip board at the nursery, it makes me nervous. What is he writing down? Is he writing about me?"—**Dusty Miller**

"I couldn't stop laughing. I loved the illustrations. I loved the stories, but the real belly-laughers were the customer comments—maybe one was mine."—**Daphne Odora**

"Beware! Once you start, you won't be able to put this book down until you've read the whole thing. It sounds like a fun nursery to be a tree in."—**Ray Woodash**

"European nurseries are so boring. After reading this book, I simply must come to the States and visit this wonderful nursery. I want to meet the man who has saved the earth from extraterrestrials so many times."—**Countess Helene von Stein**

"At first I was completely bamboozled and thought the stories really happened. What a great imagination! It was heavenly."—**Nan Dina**

"I was going to say that the illustrations were the best part of this book, but I didn't want to hurt Don's feelings. Too bad. They were fantastic!"—**Cary Opteris**

"I have asked Don dozens of dumb questions over the years, so it was with some trepidation that I read the customer quips and questions. Looks like I dodged a bullet."—**Leon Otis**

"I loved Grafting Class. Big Lou sounds like my cousin, Marcello, in the Bronx. He's a businessman, too. If ya know what I mean."—**Sal Via Apiana**

"After I read Don's book, I immediately called the nursery and asked the dumbest question I could think of. Now I want to know when the next book is coming out. I'm pretty sure I'll be in it."—**Sam Bucus**

Made in the USA
San Bernardino, CA
17 December 2018